REMEMBER RACHEL

When Martin Warbeck killed Rachel Shea in 1883 he felt she richly deserved it after her clumsy attempts at blackmail. Although someone had seen him, no one reported the murder and twenty years later, Martin was the owner of a beautiful country house, with a rich wife and a beautiful mistress. In the space of a few months, however, he loses all he possesses. Is Fate to blame, or does someone from the past have a score to settle? Someone who has watched and waited for the perfect moment. If he retaliates, can Martin get away with murder again?

REMEMBER RACHEL

REMEMBER RACHEL

by
Elizabeth Ann Hill

Magna Large Print Books
Long Preston, North Yorkshire,
England.

British Library Cataloguing in Publication Data.

Hill, Elizabeth Ann
 Remember Rachel.

A catalogue record for this book is
available from the British Library

ISBN 0-7505-1352-7

First published in Great Britain by Severn House Publishers
Ltd., 1997

Published in Large Print 1999 by arrangement with Severn
House Publishers Ltd.

Magna Large Print is an imprint of
Library Magna Books Ltd.
Printed and bound in Great Britain by
T.J. International Ltd., Cornwall, PL28 8RW.

Sometimes, in still weather, when the surface of the lake lay smooth and glossy green, he imagined he could see her face staring up at him through the clear water. That insolent, mocking face. There on the bottom, among the stones and the drifting weed, she winked at him and laughed.

And then the image would shiver, ripple and dissolve into thrashing foam and he could see his hands in her hair, dragging her under, hear the coughing screams as she tried to break surface and see her fingers, arms streaked with mud and weed, clawing at his clothes—until the gradual silence fell and he knew with growing panic that he had gone too far and there was now much more than the money to lose.

Now and again he would come to this small clearing between quiet woods and the water's edge, because it happened here and because nowhere else did it seem quite real. Even after so many long years he had only to come to this place and the memory would return with dreadful clarity of the day he drowned Rachel Shea.

His grey mare snorted and stamped a little with impatience but the man on her back took no notice, absorbed in the memory and the question that always came with it. Where did they go? The old woman and the boy—her mother and brother—where? For nearly twenty years the question had hovered in an unquiet corner of his mind. Always, when he remembered Rachel, there came a sense of something suspended and incomplete. Her murder passed and was concealed with a kind of unnatural ease, which left him thankful but unsettled. Now, as on so many other occasions, his thoughts began to wander their well-trodden way back to the beginning, to a day when he was twenty-four ...

PART ONE—JUNE, 1882

ONE

Martin Warbeck finished his glass of port and smiled to himself. It reminded him of Lucy Vincent—rich, full-bodied and flavoursome. Or so he imagined. He hadn't actually made the conquest yet but there was cause for optimism and he toyed with the idea of taking a ride to Stennack after lunch to see the delectable Lucy. She was plump and affable and, most important, she admired him. Martin liked to be admired, especially by women. It was not because he felt any respect or liking for them, but he loved the adulation. It was such fun and, he believed, no more than his due. Females who displayed indifference to him filled Martin with an almost vicious need to 'cut the bitch down to size.' They were, after all, supposed to be impressed. His contempt for women however was merely a symptom of a more deep-seated disregard for people in general—a trait well-concealed for the most part but occasionally glimpsed by a relative or close friend when Martin let the charm slip.

He got up to pour himself some more port, found the decanter all but empty and swore under his breath. He would have to get it filled before the old man came in. Gordon Warbeck couldn't bear to see either of his sons drinking. He kept the stuff in the house for the benefit of guests and chance callers, but expected his family to follow his own teetotal example. Martin was well aware that his father didn't like him and he knew better than to aggravate the situation by getting caught at the port.

Gordon was one of the perceptive few who mistrusted Martin's charm. The same suspicious nature had proved useful in his business ventures and saved him from any major investment blunders, but there was still a lot he didn't know about his eldest son. Try as he might, Gordon found it impossible to like him. The old man's main complaints were Martin's aversion to work and his expensive habit of backing losers at the races—neither of which showed any signs of reform.

Martin took the cellar keys from his father's desk and strolled out of the study, across the coloured tiles of the hall and down to the kitchen stairway. It was fortunate for him that his mother did all the ordering for the house, including the wines and spirits, for Gordon would certainly have noticed the disappearance of so much port. If Hannah Warbeck was aware of her son's little raids she had never mentioned it.

At the top of the cellar steps Martin paused, listening. There were voices from the kitchen—his mother's voice and that of a younger woman. It was not the pert, bouncy tone of Dorcas, the Warbecks' parlourmaid, but a cool, matter-of-fact voice which he didn't recognise.

'A shawl?'

'Yes, dear. I do realise the enormous amount of work involved, but there's no rush to have it ready and naturally you'll

15

be well paid. If you tell me what is necessary I will supply the thread and any other materials you want. Even if it takes a year I'm sure it will be worthwhile.'

'Aye, of course, I'll be pleased to do it, Mrs Warbeck. Is the collar as you wanted?'

'It's beautiful, Rachel, I'm delighted with it.'

Curious, Martin slipped the keys into his pocket and pushed open the kitchen door. A girl stood there with her back to him; a small, trim figure in a green linsey-woolsey skirt, with a black blouse and faded pinafore. A gleaming fall of copper-coloured hair reached almost to her waist. The effect was both startling and pleasing for he seldom saw a grown woman with her hair worn loose.

'Martin?' His mother put down the lace collar she had been examining. 'Are you looking for me?'

Martin hesitated. 'Uh, tea. I wanted some tea but I can't find Dorcas and she hasn't answered the bell.'

The girl turned to look at him. He

16

supposed her to be about nineteen or twenty, which was an overestimate, for Rachel was just turned sixteen. Pretty? No, he wouldn't call her that, but good-looking, yes. The mouth was humorous and well-shaped and the green eyes had a directness in their gaze that was uncommon in a cottage girl. There was something about Rachel's manner and bearing that was both challenge and invitation, a suggestion of subtle cheek.

'Dorcas is in the sitting-room, dear,' his mother said.

Martin wasn't listening. He was still staring at the girl, who, unperturbed, stared back. Hannah looked amused.

She said, 'Rachel, this is my eldest son.'

Martin nodded to her with a faint smirk. 'Hello, Rachel.'

''Morning, sir.' She bobbed him a perfunctory curtsey and turned back to Hannah. 'Well, I'll be off now then, Mrs Warbeck. If you'll choose whichever thread you fancy I'll make a start on your shawl. I can work with almost anything, as you know.'

She took the little envelope Hannah gave her in payment for the lace collar, picked up her basket of mushrooms and disappeared through the back door and across the herb garden.

'I'll make the tea for you,' offered Hannah. 'Martin? Are you listening?'

'What? Oh, no, don't bother. It's nearly lunchtime anyway.'

'Rachel's a lovely girl, isn't she?'

'Mmph, not bad,' he allowed and then, remembering the port, excused himself and headed once more for the cellar.

His mother picked up the collar again, admiring the girl's handiwork. Hannah was a kind woman, unprepared to believe ill of anyone, much less speak it. She was generous and even-tempered, if slightly out of touch with reality. In one way she had been fortunate, for her naivete had never been shattered, had never led her into trouble, but served almost as armour-plating against the unpleasant things in life. Faced with the dark side of human nature, Hannah made excuses for it, simply disbelieved it or failed to understand. It was a trait which Gordon found both endearing and exasperating.

Above all, Hannah was proud of her sons. At twenty-four Martin was just over six feet tall. He was witty and attractive and she saw his irresponsibility as a passing thing, easily cured by a good wife; something that would vanish when he applied his considerable intelligence to a career. She was not alarmed that his younger brother was already making headway as a reporter on the local newspaper while Martin showed no sign of interest in any kind of job. Hannah's critical faculties, always limited, were non-existent with regard to her own family.

The marked difference in temperament between her two sons had been obvious since their childhood. Martin had been a strange, impassive child, never afflicted with the nightmares and imaginings that had kept his younger brother wakeful and wide-eyed in the dark, night after night. There were no alligators under Martin's bed; no malevolent, scaly creatures with talons and teeth skulked behind his wardrobe; no spectres, no crawling horrors, no murderers. He was also indifferent to criticism unless it was accompanied by some kind of punishment. Hannah always liked to think of the boy as self-possessed. His father preferred 'cold-blooded'.

Their other son, Neil, was unremarkable to look at and six years Martin's junior. Now eighteen, he was a background person, a slightly boring young man, with a few adolescent, sandy whiskers struggling to become a moustache. He suffered the odd bout of ill-temper, sometimes managed a mild joke and accepted life just as it was—unspectacular. Unlike his popular and discontented brother, Neil had a job. He even liked it. Martin couldn't stand him but was careful not to show it.

Having replaced the port, Martin stood by the study window, thinking. Rachel. Yes, he remembered now. The Shea girl, the lacemaker. These were the people who had moved into the old cottage on the northern edge of the woods. They were not locals but came from somewhere up north. It was 1882 and thousands of agricultural workers with their families were leaving the countryside for the better life they thought awaited them in the towns and cities. More often than not they were going from bad conditions to worse.

Industry had bypassed this part of the country and he wondered why the Sheas had settled for a small market town when other poor people believed so firmly that the city meant wealth. But then the Sheas were not farm workers.

Cassie Shea was a widow, a handloom weaver—one of a dwindling few now, pushed out by the coming of the great mills which were part of the industrial rash that was breaking out all over England. It amazed Martin that she could find any buyers for her homespun woollen cloth. Of course she did take in sewing too, which added a few precious shillings to their weekly income.

Her daughter Rachel did a little weaving but made most of her living from the lace she fashioned for the well-to-do ladies of Meadstock. Word had soon got round that the Shea girl had a fine way with lace. Her work was delicate, the patterns unusual, and it became almost prestigious to own some—which enabled her to charge a bit extra.

Lastly there was the boy. A grubby, insolent urchin, known to be light-fingered (though he was never caught), who worked in Cormack's cabbage fields for the princely sum of 1s 6d a week.

Their cottage was rented from a butcher in Meadstock—something to be envied by the half-starved farm labourers and their families, dependent as they were on the goodwill or otherwise of the squire and his farmers. It was a mark, if not of prosperity, then at least of independence to rent a decent cottage from a tradesman, rather than take a leaking hovel with clay floors as provided by the more stingy landowners in the area. Seven or eight men, women and children might be huddled into one of these fearful shacks, with dirt and damp for company, so the Sheas in their dry stone cottage were comparatively well off. Furthermore, Rachel's clothes were a little more colourful than most, which caused some 'tsking' in the town, especially among the daughters of gentleman farmers. These ladies, peacocks themselves, deplored the fact that a mere cottager aspired to look attractive.

However it was not entirely out of dislike or envy that the Shea family was ignored locally. They were, above all, outsiders and the poorer people, their energies entirely consumed by the struggle to scrape together a good meal now and then, had time neither for friendship nor curiosity about strangers.

Martin Warbeck though had all the time and curiosity in the world. The girl was interesting, something different. There was none of the usual cottager's humility in her and she was attracted to him, he was certain—but of course that was only natural. What was more, Rachel Shea was uncommonly clean and fresh, which, he thought, was quite novel for one of her level. The coy prudery of his own class and the complete absence of hygiene amongst the village girls made Rachel Shea a very attractive prospect—for a little fun, that is.

Nothing more of course.

He took his ride to Stennack as planned but Lucy Vincent's prattlings that day fell mainly on deaf ears, for his mind was entirely on the Shea girl. Lucy was dull. They were all dull. Conversation was the same in most middle-class households: stilted and predictable. True to form, Lucy's chat ran from food to the weather to her Uncle's gallstones and finally a resumé of the Reverend Prinkett-Styles's latest strident attack on sin from the pulpit of St Mark's. Martin eyed her coldly as she gabbled. He was disappointed in Lucy. Her daring stopped short with a peck on the cheek and he had hoped for rather more. Martin had first sampled sex at the age of seventeen and had never been able to get enough since. In fact he had barely got any. Victorian society fixed a stern watch on such things and even his most adoring lady friends kept their legs crossed and their bosoms to themselves.

He left at around four, feeling evil-tempered and bored with his respectable circle of friends, longing for some kind of change. A trip to London was impossible on his allowance, which he considered miserly. The fact was that, no matter what Gordon gave him, it could never be enough and it galled him to know that Neil was better off for cash than he was. The idea of taking a job appalled Martin and so he was permanently short of money and always borrowing.

As he rode home his thoughts turned back to Rachel Shea, seeking some excuse, some not-too-obvious means of seeing her again. The answer, simple and convenient, came almost at once. As soon as she had chosen it he would deliver Hannah's thread to the cottage.

TWO

'How much?'

The young man hesitated.

'I said how much?'

Martin fidgeted, shifting uneasily from foot to foot. He was never comfortable in his father's presence, least of all when the interview concerned money.

'Twenty-nine pounds, roughly,' he mumbled.

The air was charged with disapproval as the old man settled back thoughtfully in his chair. He was short and broad-featured, with a glacial grey-eyed stare that grew even colder and more fixed whenever he suspected deceit.

'More than Dorcas earns in a year,' he said acidly.

Martin couldn't see what that had to do with anything.

'Well?' prodded Gordon.

Martin cleared his throat. 'I was hoping you might, um, well, you know—an advance?' He waited while the silence grew longer and the old man frowned at the blotter on his desk, considering.

'On what?' he asked finally, although there could only be one answer.

'My allowance.'

'As usual. Somehow you never quite manage to catch up, do you Martin? Your allowance is invariably spent six months in advance.' He leaned forward suddenly and jabbed a warning finger towards his son. 'The only reason I continue to make these little "loans" is that I am not prepared to have it said that my son owes money to every bookmaker and tradesman in the county.'

Martin glanced at him sullenly from under his eyebrows.

'It's just this once ...'

'That's quite correct, young man. It will be just this once, for this is the last—and I emphasise "last"—time that I will lend you anything for any purpose. We'll ignore what you have borrowed so far and carry on with your allowance as normal, but there will be no more extras. I've given up hope of your ever repaying anything, unless by some miracle you decide to take a job. Does that appeal to you, hmm? I'd have no trouble in finding you a position.'

Martin was silent, his eyes wandering everywhere but avoiding his father.

'No. I thought not.'

'If you'll excuse me I've got a lunch appointment in town ...'

'Yes, go on, go on.' The old man waved him irritably away and watched the study door close behind his son. The boy always took off like a hare when work was mentioned, or made excuses or changed the subject. He was a huge disappointment, lacking any of the characteristics Gordon admired in a man.

Before he retired Warbeck had been a master-builder, a moral, church-going man who would work himself into the ground for a chance of advancement. Within himself Gordon still harboured memories of his childhood, the interminable hours spent pasting matchboxes at 1d a gross.

These old images visited him at odd moments of the day to remind him who he was and it seemed to the old man, just before he drifted off to sleep at night, that he could so easily wake one morning to find himself back in mean streets. At this moment though he was thinking that a taste of the farm labourer's life would do Martin an awful lot of good.

The Warbecks were comparatively new to the district. They came from Bristol, where Gordon had made his money and met Hannah, whom he had married late in life, being almost twenty years her senior.

He had bought this house in late 1880. It formed part of the estate of a lesser member of the gentry, ruined by the bad harvest of 1879, who had sold everything and taken a tearful wife and two fractious daughters to Baden-Baden to live more modestly. The property had been divided between several buyers and Warbeck had got the house, lake and surrounding woodlands.

Forest Rift was so called for the simple reason that it stood in a clearing on the southern edge of the lake, a gap hewn out of the thick woodland which grew right down to the banks of Rowan Water. Its design was a kind of gentle chaos, with gables and doorways placed seemingly at random and a glass conservatory extending right along the eastern side. This was a house of warm colours and dark polished wood, airy in summer and snug when the cold came, without the wall-to-wall ornaments, photographs and sundry junk which festooned most middle-class households. Paintings and books lined the walls and shelves, and almost every room carried its own distinctive perfume of lavender or polish, baking or soap or burning apple logs. It was very countrified and nestled in its clearing like a chestnut in a shell, completely in harmony with the surrounding woods.

Rowan Water was not especially deep—perhaps thirty-five feet in the middle—but it shelved steeply in places. Near the shore grew large patches of duckweed and cattail. The lake stretched for nearly a mile from the Warbeck house on the south side to the northern end where the woods began to thin out and the narrow forest path widened into a track smooth and broad enough for a pony and trap. Two miles along this road lay Meadstock, a market town of some two thousand inhabitants, small but growing yearly as shops, schools and banks sprang up, together with superior housing for gentlefolk.

Life was no longer so rural. Everything and everybody was changing. The old clear-cut social order of gentry and peasantry was becoming distorted by a new breed—the middle class, with all its own subdivisions and pretences. The Warbecks were just such people. Gordon had made a great deal of money in his trade as a master-builder and as he grew older and less active he began making a few shrewd investments, so that he retired with a considerable fortune—more than enough to realise a lifelong dream of a secluded home with peace and good air.

Because it was more than a mile off the main highway Forest Rift saw few of the wandering tradesmen who passed through the towns. There was of course the sweep and a boy who came sometimes to clean shoes and sharpen any knives that needed it—a service for which Hannah paid him 4d a time. There were delivery boys with necessary supplies, and the occasional gypsy, but that was all. Anyone else who called was usually a family friend.

The main access to Forest Rift was a road that branched sharply southwards away from the lake and towards Stennack, a town slightly larger than Meadstock and four miles distant. It was this road that Martin had taken, anxious to escape a discussion on a suitable career.

It annoyed him that his father always managed to turn the conversation to that unwelcome subject. After all, there was no necessity for him to work and he felt disinclined to do so, while the old man had more money than he knew what to do with. The sons of the gentry didn't have to lift a finger unless they fell on hard times, so why should he? Martin took no account of his father's working background and values. He himself had always known money, plentiful money, and the fact that the Warbecks were by no means members of the gentry did nothing to change his attitude. As long as there was sufficient cash to keep him comfortably Martin did not intend to work—ever. Anyway, there was always Neil to borrow from. The boy was dull but at least he wasn't mean. Martin grinned. Thank God for his plodding, soft-touch brother.

THREE

'Rachel, there's a man here to see you. A gentleman.'

Cassie Shea's awe-stricken face peered around the cottage door at her daughter where she knelt by the hearth, poking bits of kindling into a nearly dead fire.

'Who?'

'It's him from that house over by the lake, where the nice lady lives. The one that pays you so well.'

'Ah.' A grin spread across the girl's face and she got up, wiping the grime from her hands on the back of the green skirt.

'Aye, now what a surprise,' she purred, her tone suggesting it was no surprise at all.

'Well come on,' urged the older woman, 'you can't keep the likes of him waiting.'

The girl smoothed her hair and straightened her pinafore before sauntering outside to meet the great man.

Warbeck nodded acknowledgement to her but didn't get off his horse. He preferred to be looking down at her.

'Good-morning, Miss Shea.'

''Morning, sir. I never expected to see you—so soon.'

Martin handed down a small package to her. 'Thread,' he explained. 'I believe you are to make a shawl for my mother.'

'It's thoughtful of you to deliver it personally.'

'My pleasure.'

'Really?' The girl smiled up at him, provocation in every line and movement of her.

'Truly.'

'Aye, well, she's a kind lady. I'm always pleased to make something for her.'

'You do a lot of work for my mother?'

'A fair bit. She keeps me busy.'

'Then I assume we'll be seeing a good deal of you?' His eyes wandered over her with a familiarity which would turn his respectable lady friends crimson. Rachel didn't seem to mind. Her eyebrows lifted in mock innocence.

'I expect to see quite a lot of you too.'

The agreement was made as simply as that.

Cassie Shea, peering goggle-eyed and a trifle suspicious from the cottage window, nodded to herself, remembering a certain gentleman she had known in her youth. The great difference between Rachel and her mother was that Cassie had stood in awe of her wealthy gent and considered herself highly honoured to have attracted such a man. To Rachel sex, like death, was a great leveller and could give a measure of power to the poorest woman, provided she had a good face and body, with the wits to use them. Even so, she didn't quite appreciate just how formidable social barriers can be.

The young man's hand went to his pocket and he drew out some silver coins.

'In appreciation of your efforts, Rachel.' His smile had become a smirk.

She dropped the coins down the front of her blouse, where they lodged cosily in the ample bosom.

'You're very generous, sir, thank you.' She scuffled her left foot absently in the dust for a moment, head cocked to one side, then, 'Perhaps you'll have occasion to come this way again—in the next day or two?'

'Can you suggest some reason why I should?'

The girl shrugged. 'Oh, just because it's bracing weather. Especially round Rowan Hollow,' she added slyly.

'You think I need fresh air and exercise?'

Rachel grinned. He would have to wait awhile for the exercise—but that would make him all the keener.

'I'll expect you, then,' she half-stated, half-asked.

Martin nodded. 'Oh yes, for sure you can expect me.'

Rachel watched him go, pleased at her success. She was particular who she walked out with and the slouching village lads, rejected to the last man, reckoned she was 'hoity-toity and full of airs, silly bitch.' The fact was that Rachel enjoyed a romp with a healthy young man, provided she thought him worthy of her, and this one certainly had plenty of money. She was a fairly uncommon breed of woman in those years of Victorian prudery—one who liked sex for its own sake. And if it brought a few perks with it, well so much the better. The only other female in the district with similar appetites was the lustful Dorcas, Hannah's parlourmaid, and Martin had already had enough of her—she made far too much noise about it.

Cassie scurried over to her daughter. 'Well, what did he give you?'

Rachel fished out the coins and counted them. Ten shillings. More than enough to live on for a week. It was nothing to him of course but for the Shea family this was a small windfall. There were a few repairs needed around the cottage and perhaps now they could afford to have them done. The windows still had glass in them but some of the thatch needed replacing and the ricketty old door would never shut properly. It didn't matter too much in summer but summer wouldn't last for ever. The ten shillings would cover new blankets too and Cassie would have bought shoes for the boy but for the fact she knew he wouldn't wear them.

'Well,' said the old woman, 'I think we can afford to have bacon tonight and maybe a bit of cheese.'

Rachel's face lit up. 'Oh, yes. Barley dumplings! And bilberry pie? And elderberry wine?'

Cassie nodded. 'Yes, girl. For once we'll have a special meal.'

In the months that followed, Rachel never took offence at the secretive nature of their meetings and never again after that first occasion did he give her money. Instead he bought her presents—not every time but quite often—and she was content enough to sell the things she didn't like and keep the ones that appealed to her.

They had several haunts in the woods, where they met for frenzied, noisy coupling on the grass, and if the weather was wet, well—there was always Cormack's hayloft. Now and again he collected her at the cottage but thought it beneath his dignity to set foot inside. Occasionally, if his parents were away, he took her to the house and Rachel fancied he enjoyed the manoeuvres of sneaking her in and out as much as he liked bedding her.

Rachel managed to view the whole thing as a romantic adventure. She was lucky enough to be able to read and recalled several works of romantic fiction which assured her that all the best and truest affairs were both clandestine and ill-fated. She was, after all, only sixteen and somehow her adolescent fantasies and her worldliness made peace with each other. It was not until months later, when everything went wrong, that she really acknowledged the bald truth that he didn't want anyone to see him with her.

Martin made her laugh, he let her ride his horse and more often than not he brought a bottle of brandy or port with him and they would share it in the hayloft. As long as things remained on this footing all was well. He was her chief source of entertainment and Rachel's life seemed brighter for it. Only once did she attempt in one small way to overstep the mark. On the occasion of Hannah's birthday Rachel sent her a greetings card. Martin was furious. It took him days to calm down and his manner became stiff and distant. It didn't help for Rachel to point out that she knew his mother as one of her customers. He was incensed that she should draw attention to herself in any way and thereafter Rachel trod a little more warily.

It was eventually noticed that she accepted less work from the ladies in the town. Some speculated that Rachel's eyesight was failing after years of peering at the intricate, close patterns of her work and the time came when few of them bothered to ask her any more. Her lacemaking became gradually redundant but Rachel, who lived exclusively in the present, wasn't worried. Until, that is, she noticed that Martin's visits were becoming a little less frequent.

He came when he felt the need but there was clearly a drop in his enthusiasm. The old boredom had taken longer to set in this time but, without doubt, he was losing interest.

She was less than pleased at the prospect of losing her wealthy friend and his cash and when, in early December, Rachel's period failed for the second month to appear she realised that worse was to come. It was certainly his child, there could be no doubt, and for several days she turned it all over in her mind, seeking the best course of action.

Marry her? Oh no, she didn't suppose for one moment that he would do that. Not now. Although at the start of their relationship there had perhaps been a vague hope at the back of her mind for something like that. After all, such things were not unknown. But it was different now. She knew him better, realised that she was never more than a diversion for him. Well, that was all right. She'd had a good deal of fun herself, except that suddenly the matter was a little more serious. She was pregnant and the raising of a child costs money. For the first time Rachel felt a twinge of unease and wished she had kept her lace customers.

Whatever happened, he would have to pay some kind of maintenance for the child. He would probably be proud to, she assured herself, especially if it was a boy. For all her familiarity, Rachel didn't know Martin Warbeck very well.

'What's on your mind, girl? Why so subdued, eh? I've not seen you laugh for nearly a week.'

'Do I have to go round with a daft smile stuck on my face then?'

'And your temper's none too lovable either. There has to be a reason.'

Rachel went on doggedly struggling to repair an old wicker basket which served them for both shopping and collecting firewood. It was close to falling apart and as fast as her shaking fingers attempted to patch one hole another would open elsewhere. The red hair cascaded forward, hiding her face, and she muttered irritably about always making do.

'Look at me!' demanded Cassie.

Reluctantly the girl raised her eyes to

her mother and swiftly looked away again. 'Don't natter at me, Ma. I'm busy.'

'I want to know.'

Rachel bit her lip. It was pointless to deny what time would eventually make obvious and anyway the relationship always had Cassie's approval.

'He doesn't see you so often now, does he?' pressed her mother.

'Why should I care?'

'Now that's a stupid question, Rachel. A catch like him ...'

'Catch!' The girl flung the basket away. 'Oh, have some sense, Ma. Men like him don't marry my sort. They marry rich.'

'There's nothing wrong with you. You're good enough to draw his attention, good enough to ...'

'Not for much longer.'

'Has he said so?'

'Not yet, but he will when he knows.'

'Knows? What is there to know?'

Rachel sighed. 'Can't you guess, Ma? It's not so unusual, after all.'

Sudden understanding overtook Cassie.

'Oh, Rachel. Are you expecting, girl? Is that it?'

'Aye, that's it. Now you know.'

Cassie got up and paced around, distractedly rubbing her hands on her pinafore. 'Will he marry you?' she asked finally.

'I doubt it.'

There was a moment's silence, then Cassie shook her head.

'I don't know where we'll find the money to feed another child, now that you've lost your customers. Are you sure he won't ...?'

'Pretty sure. But I believe he may help us out. He can afford it and he knows how little we have. A few shillings a week mean nothing to him. He's got plenty—I mean, look at all the things he bought me.'

'I hope you're right. What you must realise is that we're talking of a fairly large sum, taken over a period of years. Paying for a child costs more than a few trinkets, Rachel, and you must tread softly with him. You're in no position to make demands.' A worried frown darkened her face. 'He may not even admit it's his. People will wonder who the father is and I doubt he'll want it known. Rich folks don't like to be embarrassed.'

'Embarrassed!' exclaimed Rachel. ''Tis me that's going to walk around looking like a suet dumpling for the next few months, me they're going to stare at, point at. He's had his fun and he's not leaving me to face this by myself, just to save his dignity. Anyway,' she started to laugh, 'Martin fancies his reputation as a ladies' man. He might welcome a spot of notoriety.'

Cassie pointed a warning finger at her daughter. 'Now it's you who's being naive. A man can hint at his exploits and be admired but if you think he will openly admit this kind of responsibility you're mistaken. I hoped at one time he might marry you. Now the best we can hope for is cash to get by on. You've not played your hand very well, girl. Still, what's done is done. You're very young and you have no guile.'

Rachel said nothing. She had never

really expected more than a bit of fun, never laid any long-term schemes, and anyway Cassie herself had failed to land a gentleman, so she was in no position to criticise. Rachel knew enough about life to realise that money most often married more money. Her marriage fantasies, never taken seriously, had vanished with the greetings card incident.

'When will you see him?'

'These days I never know. It used to be regular but not any more.'

'You'll tell him as soon as possible?'

'Of course.'

'Remember what I say now, walk softly and maybe he'll be generous.'

'I'm not going to beg,' retorted Rachel hotly. 'He has a duty now and he'll have to face it.'

'You've got a lot to learn, girl,' muttered the old woman, 'an awful lot.'

Sitting on a pile of straw with her back to the wall, Rachel watched him hitch up his pants and tuck in his shirt. A week had passed and still she had not broken the news. It was to be today. It couldn't wait any longer but an odd sense of tension made her reluctant to speak, made her postpone her announcement. It was rare that Rachel's nerve failed her but this was proving more difficult than expected. Instinct said 'tread carefully,' but there was no way to wrap up the hard fact of her pregnancy to make it more presentable. This secret was like an aching tooth—the thing would have to come out eventually. She took a deep breath.

'I'm pregnant.' The words came in a high, nervous burst and seemed to hang in the air, waiting to be cut down.

He turned slowly, his shirt still half unbuttoned and the necktie crumpled in his hand, which closed rigidly into a fist. His hazel eyes looked almost yellow as the pupils shrank and the lines around his mouth drew down, hostile and taut.

'Did you hear? I'm pregnant.' Her tone was steadier this time. No use to waver now.

His eyes flicked down to her belly and back to her face. One dark eyebrow lifted to convey indifference.

'Why are you telling me? It's not mine.'

'Of course it's yours. I, I've been meaning to tell you for a week or two.'

The other eyebrow lifted to join its twin. 'Don't be silly, Rachel.' He sounded calm enough, not at all angry, but there was that in his face and manner from which she should have taken warning.

It seemed he was going to argue. Rachel felt a quiver of anger. It had occurred to her that he might try this but she had thought it more likely that he would offer to pay up straight away to keep the affair as quiet as possible. It was part of her 'everything will be all right somehow' attitude to life and she felt a stab of panic at the thought that now, when she was in deep trouble, this might not be so.

She got to her feet, colour rising with temper. Her clothes were still undone and she fumbled to straighten them and thereby gain a bit of dignity. Martin began to laugh. Other people's discomfiture always tickled his sense of humour.

'Of course it's damn well yours.'

'Not necessarily.'

Rachel was furious, with him and herself, knowing she had lost control far too quickly. His grin grew broader. Martin was enjoying this immensely. It was a little extra bonus, some unexpected fun.

'I'm not asking you, I'm telling you. You'll have to provide for it.'

'Certainly not. After all,' he went on, 'the father could be any of a score of men. I'm sure your adventures are not confined to me, love, any more than mine are to you. I assume you've singled me out as the wealthiest but I've no intention of paying for any brat which is probably someone else's.'

Rachel gasped. 'But you know, you know quite well that I haven't been seeing anyone else.'

'Do I?'

Of course he did know. His very conceit assured him she was right and that he was the only possible father. Martin, who disliked the idea of sharing a woman, would not have wanted it any other way

51

but, under the circumstances, he was not going to admit it.

It was beginning to dawn on Rachel just how badly she had misjudged him. She had seen him charming, amusing and sometimes vulgar, but never cruel. Never before. No, she wouldn't expect him to be pleased at the news but surely he was gentleman enough to settle the matter graciously—generously? Poor, silly Rachel.

'I do hope you don't imagine I would marry you,' he went on. 'My plans include a banker's daughter from Stennack—which leaves you out of the running unless you have a secret fortune somewhere. You won't get a penny out of me, Rachel. The misfortune is entirely yours and you can do with the brat as you wish. I have no interest in offspring, mine or anyone else's. And anyway, surely you accepted this risk before you got involved with me? I assumed you knew what you were doing. It's no good to come bleating to me now.'

He was right. She knew he was right and

felt a stab of shame for her own stupidity. But the thing was done. The baby was his and surely he felt some interest in it at least? Rachel struggled with her temper for a moment, her mind working hastily, still not prepared to give up.

'I wonder how your father will feel about it,' she said at last. 'Rumour says he's a high-minded, church-going man and that you're not the favourite of his sons. I hear he disapproves of you already. Well, things could get worse, I dare say. Your life could be a little chillier, less safe and well provided. When he hears ...'

For one satisfying moment she thought she had won. as the arrogance faded from his face to be replaced by panic. But only one moment. Rachel backed off a few steps, sensing something more dangerous in him than ridicule or contempt, then screamed as the palm of his hand caught the side of her face with a sickening smack, flinging her head to one side, then swiping it back again with a second blow to the other cheek.

'Bitch!' The word exploded like steam

through his clenched teeth as Rachel, her sense of balance lost, swayed ready to keel over. He grasped her left arm and the collar of her blouse, slamming her back against one of the upright wooden beams of the loft.

'My old man wouldn't spare five minutes to listen to you.'

'What are you so frightened of then?'

'Frightened? Me? Don't flatter yourself. How do you think he would react if you tried to tell him his son and heir consorts with a shabby little baggage like you?'

But he was frightened. Sweat was running off his seething face and Rachel knew she had touched a nerve. Martin was afraid of his father. This was the way to twist his arm.

'I will,' she hissed. 'I'll give him a graphic account of all the times in Rowan Hollow and all the times you took me to the house and especially,' she ended with satisfaction, 'all the things you've said about him.'

He jerked her head back with a crack against the beam.

'Pay me,' she screamed into his face. 'Just pay me. I can't see why you grudge me a few shillings a week. You lose enough on one horse to keep me and mine for a year. All I want is enough to feed it and buy it some clothes. That's the least of what you owe ...'

The blackness seemed to whoosh round from the back of her head, shot with bright flashes, to blot out her vision, as his fist landed a shocking blow in her stomach and she sagged, rasping for breath, onto the wooden planking. He stood over her for a moment. She could sense him looking down at her and then 'Stupid bitch,' he muttered. Snatching up his jacket, he clattered down the shaky old stairs to the floor of the barn and stalked out through the door. A moment later she heard the thudding vibration of retreating hooves and struggled to sit up. Rachel had miscalculated badly.

There was a change in Martin Warbeck. Neil and Hannah first noticed it at dinner that night. He was preoccupied and had lost his appetite—which caused anxiety in his mother, suspicion in his father.

Martin's mind dwelt constantly on the fear that Rachel might be as good as her word and inform the old man that he was soon to be a grandparent. She might see him in town or send him a note. The suspense was gruelling.

Hannah, who noticed that her son was always hovering round whenever the doorbell rang or the post came, supposed he was waiting to hear from some nice girl he'd met, while his father developed the feeling that Martin was keeping an eye on him. He seemed uncommonly interested in where Gordon had been each day and who he had met. This went on for nearly a fortnight as the loss of his idle, comfortable way of life hung over Martin's neck like a hatchet, held in the small hand of a country girl.

At the cottage, meanwhile, Cassie Shea watched her daughter's brooding face as, day after day, the marks of a mind busy with angry schemes were stamped there.

If anything, the beating had made Rachel more determined than ever to get some kind of redress. But what? And how? The feeling of helpless rage was nigh intolerable and Cassie gave her little comfort.

'Let it lie, girl, unless you want another trouncing—or something even worse. What sympathy do you think you'll get from a narrow-minded old man like Warbeck? Aye, maybe he would believe you but do you think he would part with one halfpenny? More likely he'd pronounce it God's judgement on you, and punishment that you struggle to bring up the child alone.'

'His grandchild?'

'Well, you can't exactly prove that, can you? And if you make trouble for your fine Martin Warbeck you may expect he will come after you again. That's a violent man, for all his lofty manners.'

'You've made me this same, stupid speech a dozen times,' snapped the girl. 'If you'd had the ill luck to get a child from your own fine gent so many years back I suppose you'd thank him kindly and never think he owed you anything? Or perhaps you'd not tell him at all but do the noble thing and take the burden entirely on yourself?'

She was almost yelling at the older woman, who gazed steadily back at her and fought a tempting urge to tell her daughter yes, that was exactly what she did, and that Rachel had the fine gentleman's eyes and his walk and the same stubborn, head-on attitude to life.

The girl snatched up her lacework and began furiously plying the bobbins, her mouth pursed with temper.

'There is something else that worries me,' continued Cassie. 'The child—what if it looks like him? What if it has his features, his colouring? In a year or two the likeness might become obvious, awkward. How do you think he would feel about that? I don't doubt it has crossed his mind already.'

'Well that surely is the proof we need. I could take it along to show old man Warbeck.'

'You think Martin would allow that?'

Rachel's face clouded as Cassie's meaning sank in.

'You don't mean he would harm it?' She laughed nervously. 'Oh come on, Ma. It's as much his as mine. Half Warbeck.'

'Rachel, he's already made it quite clear how he feels—isn't it enough that he ill-treated you? I'm surprised you didn't miscarry after that walloping. And how do you know the child will be all right ...?'

'Oh, don't, Ma. I'm worried enough already.'

'Would you mind if you did lose it?'

Rachel nodded mutely. It was hardly rational, she thought, to want it under the circumstances, but all the same she did.

'Hmm. Well, there's enough been done already,' continued Cassie. 'The best thing you can do is keep out of his way and hope this will blow over. You're rash, Rachel, and you never learn, never stop to think before you do something that's dangerous or ill-advised. You take heed of me this time and leave him alone.'

Rachel accepted this criticism, acknowledged its truth and promptly forgot it.

FOUR

It became gradually apparent to Martin that Rachel's threat was an empty one. Weeks and months passed and he heard no more from her. Once, in April, he saw her in Meadstock, conspicuously pregnant, and she had crossed the street to avoid him, which suited Martin very well.

The more viciously moral of Rachel's remaining lady customers no longer required her skills and a few coarse tradesmen derived lewd humour from her condition. The opinions of the townspeople were a matter of indifference to her, stupid and small-minded as they were. What did hurt was the knowledge that she herself had been stupid and all the regret was based on her complete misinterpretation of Martin's character.

Gradually the Shea family became even less accepted in Meadstock, more withdrawn and close between themselves, for Rachel gave short shrift to the prudes and the meddlers, the shocked and the patronising, until she was utterly unpopular. Speculation on the possible father of her embarrassment was replaced in mid-May by the even spicier revelation that the parson's wife came from a whorehouse in Bristol, where he had ventured to save souls and, in a moment's fleshly weakness, stayed for a free sample. When morning dawned in all its grey horror marriage had seemed the only adequate form of atonement. Thereafter he and Mrs Prinkett-Styles had settled for what they thought was rural anonymity in Meadstock—which was foolish of them, for there's nowhere less anonymous than a small town.

It was near the end of August when Martin next encountered Rachel, on her way to Forest Rift with Hannah's newly finished shawl. She was breezing along the woodland footpath on this balmy morning, wearing her best pink and white cotton dress and a straw sun-bonnet. It was bright and cool in the woods, a haven from the summer heat, garlanded with ivy and studded with toadstools, spiced with the light, damp smells of loam and wild herbs, leaf mould and wet bark. She felt fine that day, with an airy sense of well-being—until she met with Martin Warbeck.

Rachel stopped warily as he motioned his horse across the path to block her way. He saw straightaway that she had had her child and he was curious to know more about it. Neither spoke for some moments and the flatness of her expression told him nothing.

'It appears I'm now a father.' He made paternity sound like a disease.

The girl's eyes fixed on him, stony green. She didn't answer. Worry was writ large on his face. It showed through the arrogance and treated Rachel to a moment of satisfaction.

Martin's hands twisted the reins and his wide mouth drew down in annoyance. He was loath to show any concern but Rachel was clearly not going to volunteer any information.

'What is it then? A female? Another like you? Or a boy?'

'What difference does it make to you?'

'Mere curiosity. I suppose it has red hair?'

Rachel grinned. 'You want to know if it looks like you.'

He fidgeted awkwardly at this. She was too shrewd and too calm for comfort—as if she had an ace up her sleeve.

'And does it?'

She considered her reply and the silence lengthened, broken only by the dull, tearing sound of his horse cropping the grass beside the path.

'Well?' he prodded. 'Perhaps I should come and see for myself? It's my fatherly duty, after all.'

A haggard look suddenly crossed her face, as if he had touched on something very painful. 'Fatherly duty? It's a bit late for that.'

'Which means?'

The hollow look deepened. 'It was a boy,' she said starkly, 'stillborn.'

Martin searched her face for signs of

deceit and found the same dull stare. 'Are you sure?'

'What a stupid question,' responded the girl.

His features relaxed and a trace of humour appeared.

'And why was that, Rachel? You bungle everything, don't you?'

She experienced a flaming urge to spit at him but fought it down.

'You know damn well why. Is it surprising, after the way you treated me?'

He shrugged. 'It may have been my fault but there are many reasons why these things happen. My mother lost one, you know, a year before I was born.'

'What a pity she didn't lose you.'

Martin was too relieved to be angry at that. The threat was over. There was no child. He felt suddenly jovial, he wanted to celebrate. Hardened as she was, Rachel was stunned by the sheer nerve of what came next.

'Well, Rachel, I expect you're delighted to be rid of such an encumbrance, hmm?'

'Bastard,' she muttered quietly.

'Yes, it was, wasn't it?' retorted Martin brightly. 'Rather a mercy it didn't live to face the social stigma.'

Rachel swallowed hard. God, he was repellent.

Martin leaned confidingly down to her. 'Would you welcome a little fun—for old times' sake? My parents are leaving for Bristol in a few hours. They'll be away till tomorrow noon, collecting dear sister Celia from that idiotic finishing school of hers. I'm sure you remember your way around. You know where my room is.'

A slow frown creased her forehead as his suggestion sank in. His cheek was breathtaking but she checked herself on the brink of an abusive reply as the germ of an idea, tingling with bright possibilities, sprang into her mind.

To Martin's satisfaction the girl's face softened into the old expression of lecherous humour and the green eyes shone with what he took to be a renewed fancy for himself. It never for an instant occurred to him that she might have an ulterior motive. Such was his vanity. She had, after all, been deprived of his attentions for a long time and this was a woman who needed a man.

She stalled for a moment. 'Do you seriously think I would take up with you again? After ...?'

'Rachel, you tried to blackmail me, didn't you? But I'm prepared to forget that if you'll take it like a good loser.'

'Be a sport, eh?' Her words were vibrant with sarcasm. She understood very well that women and horse-racing were two sides of the same coin to him, all sporting entertainment, to be taken lightly just as long as he didn't lose.

'Certainly and I'll, uh, be a little more careful this time.'

'Good of you.'

'I'll leave the kitchen door unlocked after eleven tonight. I know you have the sense to tread quietly.'

'What about the maid?'

'I'll give Dorcas the evening off. She has plenty of friends in town and Neil goes to bed at ten, so you won't run into him. Will you be there?'

Rachel seemed to consider for a moment, although the decision was already made.

'Possibly,' she purred, reaching up to draw a finger thoughtfully along his thigh. 'Now I do have business with your mother and I'm late already.'

He moved his horse aside and she brushed past. There was a spring in her step which he imagined was happy anticipation. And so it was.

'I don't intend to go through this with you again,' Gordon snapped. 'Your mother and I have a train to catch, besides which I've already made the position perfectly clear. There will be no more loans. Whatever you've lost you'll have to find for yourself—that's if you're capable of doing anything for yourself.'

'How much do you need, dear? I can ...' began Hannah.

'No you can't and you won't,' said her husband firmly.

'But if it's to buy a present for Celia ...'

Gordon snorted. 'What kind of present costs that much? And if I gave him the money—which I would never see again—then the present would come from me, not him. For God's sake, Hannah, he doesn't want it for Celia. They don't even get on with each other.'

'Peace offering,' said Martin sullenly, 'that's all.'

'It was a kind thought, dear,' consoled his mother and Gordon groaned, exasperated by Hannah's blinkered good faith.

'Look, I've got to have that money,' his son said urgently. 'This is positively the last time. I really do need it, desperately.'

A dry smile crossed Gordon's fleshy face and his pale eyes gleamed.

'Well, desperation can reveal all kinds of hidden resources in us, Martin. I know all about that. It's what ...'

'Put me where I am today.' The familiar words sounded in Martin's mind before his father finished speaking. How many times had he heard that? It was one of Gordon's favourites. He loved to reiterate on his struggles, his climb from the depths, his hard work and ingenuity, and it made Martin sick. All of it was true of course but Gordon loved to dwell on it, like some kind of martyrdom.

'We'd better go, Gordon,' Hannah said hastily. 'We've less than forty minutes to catch that train.'

'Yes, come on then.' He stopped at the door and glanced back at Martin who stood glowering by the fireplace.

'Perhaps by the time we return you'll have found some solution to your plight, eh? I shall watch with interest.'

'I'm sure I will,' retorted his son defiantly.

The old man laughed and ushered Hannah out into the hall.

'I damn well will,' Martin repeated to himself although he didn't know how. There were times when he loathed his father and this was definitely one of them. Well, at least there was something to look forward to. Rachel's visit. He could take a little vengeful comfort from that. The mulish old devil would have a seizure if he knew about her. Martin chuckled. Perhaps sometime he would have the pleasure of telling him.

'That's easy,' chirped Alec, grinning at his sister. 'Nobody's ever caught me.'

'That doesn't mean they won't if you get too clever and careless. Everybody knows about you and you've been accused times enough.'

The boy shrugged. 'Bet they've got plenty worth having, eh? Better than cabbages and turnips and those old buns I get in the market.'

Rachel shook him. 'For God's sake, boy. You're not going up there to pinch food. Money buys food. And clothes. And pays the rent and saves you working fourteen hours a day. How many cabbages can you stuff in those pockets, eh? How many turnips? Not enough to make it worth your effort and my risk. What you must take is any money you can find and things that we can sell. Anything small and light that looks valuable—that's if you know what valuable looks like. But I want you to understand this: you're to take nothing that looks like it belongs to the lady. I'll skin you from nose to toe if you bring back anything of hers. No necklaces or thimbles, no shoe-buckles. Never mind how pretty they are. Do you understand me?'

''Course,' sniffed the boy, 'I'm not stupid.'

Never in her life before had Rachel stolen anything more than an apple at the market or a cake at the fair. Most local cottagers did a spot of poaching but none of them looked on that as theft. Rachel felt some remorse at robbing what was, after all, Hannah's home. But Martin owed her and she could see no other way of settling the score. It would be all right, she thought, just as long as they took no personal thing of Hannah's.

The boy watched his sister as if aware of these thoughts. He had a mass of curly hair and eyes that were almost sloe-black. Alec always looked like the last standing survivor of a street fight, grimy and ragged, his bare feet grafted with dirt. He was small and wiry, which no doubt enabled him to run faster, and because he had never been caught and had no inkling of the horrors of prison Alec enjoyed his pilfering and his narrow escapes. It was just a huge joke to the boy but Cassie, knowing that luck fails all of us sooner or later, worried continually about where he was and what he might be doing.

'The place'll be locked up,' he objected.

'Sit down and I'll explain.'

He did as ordered, perching his skinny haunches on a trestle bench before the scrubbed wooden table that dominated their one-roomed cottage. Rachel put a bowl of broth and a hunk of bread in front of him and he attacked it ravenously. The cottage was cold, even in summer, and so a fire was kept burning in the great open hearth, where stood a griddle, kettle and cooking-pots, all blackened by heat and woodsmoke.

'Why do you think I'm going to the house tonight?'

The boy glanced at her from under his eyebrows with sly amusement. He knew all about life. All about Rachel and Martin Warbeck. Her pregnancy had been educational for him.

'Are you looking forward to it, sister?'

He chortled, then ducked swiftly sideways as she aimed a swipe at his ear.

'I'll leave the window unlatched,' explained Rachel. 'You know where the conservatory is?'

Alec shook his head. 'The what?'

'The glass part, stupid, where all the plants are.'

'Oh, that.' He went on devouring his supper and Rachel sat down opposite him, her face tense in the firelight, avid with mingling excitement and fear. She rarely considered consequences when embarking on any venture. She lived one step at a time, lulled by a vague confidence that all would be well.

'There's a window at the end, a round window with coloured glass, and that's the one I'll open for you. But you're not to try and get in before every light in the house is out, even if you have to wait till one or two o'clock. The conservatory leads right into the study and I bet you'll find something in there that's worth taking.'

Alec dropped his spoon in the empty

dish with a clatter and an appreciative burp.

'How am I supposed to carry all this?' he queried doubtfully.

'Well I don't know. Take a taty sack or something. Use your head. And make sure you don't break anything.'

'It's a long way to go in the dark,' muttered the boy.

'Since when were you frightened of the dark?'

Alec didn't answer. He felt suddenly uneasy, aware that Rachel had not thought things out very carefully. This was different to pinching turnips, a bit more serious. He had never gone into a big house before and this was where that man lived, the one who had walloped his sister. He realised with some discomfort that the first and most obvious culprit would be Rachel herself and that she was approaching the whole thing with more impulse than sense.

'He'll guess it was you,' he stated flatly, 'and then what will happen?'

'It could just as easily be somebody from the town—or gypsies maybe. They get the fault for everything. And anyway, he couldn't prove it, could he? Not unless you actually get caught, so make sure you don't.'

'Rachel, I'm scared. What will Ma say?'

'She won't know till it's done, now stop making obstacles.' She poked him playfully in the ribs. 'Are you really scared? Is baby fwightened then?'

He got up and went to sit by the hearth, brooding. Rachel was ignoring all the obvious dangers. She was always like that when she got her teeth into an idea—careless. Even he, longtime thief, would tread more warily with a man like Martin Warbeck.

'I don't think we should ...'

The latch clicked.

'Shut up,' she hissed, 'Ma's home.'

The boy's attention was distracted for a while because Cassie had brought him an orange and he sat down to peel it lovingly before the fire. Rachel helped herself to some broth and pondered on the necessity to have Martin tired out and unconscious by midnight. That shouldn't be difficult.

He always passed out like a light when he was finished. She remembered fleetingly how she used to enjoy it. It couldn't be the same again though. Not now. She would just have to grit her teeth and think of money.

It was several hours later when the boy lifted his head from his mattress as the latch clicked softly, there was a moment's breath of cool night air and the door closed behind his sister. He lay down again. Something like foreboding had settled on him and urged him to break his promise, stay in his bed, however angry she might be, but sometime later he himself got up and slipped noiselessly outside.

He sat beneath the trees, rubbing his foot where he had trodden on a holly leaf. The last light went out in an upstairs room and still he waited, reluctant to make a move. His heartbeat rose into frenzied jerks and he felt sick. This was not for fun, this was a crime. If he was caught they would send him to Australia, just like Uncle Timothy. Ma said the Abborry Jinnys ate Uncle Timothy—boiled him up and shared him out till there was nothing left but his ginger hair, which the chief's favourite wife made into a wig. What was more, sometimes big houses had mad people in them that were locked away during the day and let out again at night. Ma said rich people were often mad because they went soft-headed worrying about their gold and then, when they got old, their children locked them up so's they could have all the money. Oh yes, there were awful things skulking in big houses.

Stealing had never bothered Alec before but then robbing stalls at the market was rather different—it was out in the open, he knew where to run, knew all the best alleys and hidy-holes, could lose himself in the crowd. But this house was unknown territory, dark and closed in—like walking into a bear trap. All the same, it was too late to back out now. He had promised Rachel.

He scuttled around to the side of the house and padded along beside the conservatory, peering in. A variety of houseplants were ranged along the shelf just inside the glass, their brightness quenched to an insipid, spectral green by the moonlight. He reached the end and spotted the round window, slightly ajar. Stretching out a trembling hand, his fingertips touched the cold glass and gently pushed. The window was well-oiled, it gave way quietly and easily. The boy hesitated for one long moment, then heaved himself up onto the sill. Bending double, he slipped one leg cautiously inside, then wriggled through and dropped to the floor, his bare feet making the faintest thud on the cold stone.

Fumbling in his pocket, Alec found the box of matches he had brought with him. He struck one and looked swiftly around him. There was an open door to his right, with a large room beyond. That must be the study. Cautiously he crept through, pausing to strike another match when he got inside. Yes, this was it. His bright, nervous eyes took in the solid furniture and the two glass cabinets in which various items of silver and crystal twinkled. The match burned down and he had to drop it. This was no good. He needed light and he needed both hands. Perhaps it would be safe to light the gas. The heavy, velvet curtains were drawn and as long as he kept the door shut no one would see the light. Carefully Alec closed the conservatory door behind him and reached for the brackets on the wall. There was a slight 'phoomf' as the gas took light. The boy adjusted it to a low flame and turned to get a good look at the room.

It was wondrous and it was intimidating. This one room in a great house full of lovely rooms didn't belong to the world he knew, bore no resemblance to the old cottage that was home to him. How could anyone have so many lovely things? Was there really so much money in the world? He became aware of a pleasant sensation and for one moment couldn't pinpoint what it was. Then he realised, looking down, that this was the caressing touch of a fine wool carpet beneath his feet. The softness was delightful as he felt the pile crush and spring between his toes. For a while he kneaded them like a cat, his eyes darting eagerly round the room, all fear forgotten for the present. So this was a rich man's home. A cocoon of soft warmth, polished and glowing, kept clean for you, dusted and swept, heated and aired by servants in white lacy caps and aprons. What would you know of the wind shrieking outside? Why would you ever fret over rain and frost in a house like this? For such people the elements must be a triviality, a minor annoyance, never the bringers of discomfort or even death itself.

He tried out the comfy chairs, sat himself importantly behind Gordon's desk, flipped open the cigar box and took one out, sniffed it and stuck it in the corner of his mouth. He had half a mind to light it there and then but perhaps it would be wiser to save it for later. There were more pressing things to do.

Alec began trying the desk drawers, one by one. There was nothing in most of them but writing paper and books full of numbers. The top left however was locked. The boy licked his lips. It must contain something very private or very valuable. Rummaging in his pocket, he produced a length of fine, hooked wire. Lock-picking was one of his major accomplishments and this one, he was sure, would be simple.

In fact it took him fifteen minutes to open the drawer but every second of it was worthwhile. Inside, right at the back, Alec's fingers closed on a bundle of notes and his dark eyes widened in sheer awe as he realised just how much money lay in his hand. Stuffing the money in his pants pocket, the boy turned his attention to the cabinets. They would be even easier to open but—Rachel's warning flashed on his mind—perhaps those were the lady's things. They were too pretty to belong to a man and anyway Alec could only carry so much. There was one other item which simply could not be left behind. It stood on Gordon's desk and was easily the loveliest thing in the room. He picked it up and ran his fingers along the gleaming metal. Yes, this was worth coming for and Rachel wasn't going to get her hands on it either. This was for him, to make up for all the toys he never had. It was fit for a prince, this beautiful silver horse.

He suddenly remembered the time and the long trek home which lay before him. Alec reached up and turned off the gas, skittered out into the conservatory and scrambled through the open window. It was only as he ran across the grass and into the shelter of the forest that the fear returned to him. He had been inside for just over forty minutes and half of him congratulated Alec Shea on his daring. The other half trembled for what tomorrow might bring.

Retribution came sooner than that. Cassie had awoken just after one o'clock to find both her son and daughter gone and spent several panic-stricken hours awaiting their return. She caught Alec when he sneaked in with his plunder at half past four, slapped him giddy and took away his cigar. She was terrified that Rachel would not get away safely. Her thoughts bounced back and forth between fearful images of her daughter's being led away from Forest Rift in chains and her own determination to give the girl a hiding when she came home.

FIVE

Martin woke late the following morning and stretched with immense contentment as his memory replayed the events of the previous night. He hadn't had such a good time in months, he thought, blinking at the morning and noting with mild surprise the two empty wine bottles at the foot of his bed. His clothes were strewn, together with most of the bedding, across the floor and he realised with some annoyance that he would have to make the room a little more presentable before Dorcas saw it. Dorcas and her big mouth. It was nearly noon and Rachel had long gone. She had to be up and away before the household really stirred.

He swung his legs out of bed and sat up. The quick movement brought an unexpected wave of dull pain, shot with sharp twinges: the worst kind of sick headache, the kind that sends giddy spasms of nausea from head to stomach with every movement. Martin sat for some moments, unwilling to budge in case he threw up. Red wine, cheap red wine. But then he was reluctant to waste the good stuff on Rachel.

At last he eased himself upright with the greatest care and shuffled across to the mirror. He was pale, almost haggard-looking, his mouth dry and stale. He fingered the small bite mark on his left shoulder. Careless bitch. Still, no matter, no one would see it.

Outside, the stable door banged and there came the clatter of hooves as Gil walked Coriander and Damson round the yard. Warbeck went to the window and stood observing the boy with faint curiosity. How old was he? Thirteen or fourteen? Intelligent? Yes. Too intelligent for his station—an odd-jobber, chopping wood, tending the horses, fetching and carrying, repairing and errand-running. In later times or fairer circumstances he might have been a teacher or a doctor, even a barrister.

The boy had brains and the urge to learn everything he could. Once a week Gordon allowed him to go through the shelves in his study and borrow one or two books, so the boy had gleaned a passable education. The thing that hobbled him as much as any social barrier was a sibling loyalty. His elder brother, Jacob, dull-witted and backward, was also employed by the Warbecks and Gil looked after him with a kind of tolerant resignation, keeping him out of trouble and in a job. A childhood accident accounted for Jacob's condition and Gil never ceased to speculate on what he might otherwise have been. Jacob was frightened of Martin Warbeck, not for any concrete reasons of ill-treatment but through some animal sensing of dislike and contempt for himself. Gil was aware of it too, with a resentment both defensive and hostile.

Martin shrugged. The boys were kept well enough, with good food and housing. Gil had nothing to complain about. And he had a rare way with horses, always able to get the best from them. If there was anything Martin cared for as much as himself it was horses. Someday perhaps he would have his own stables and breed them. Someday, when he got his inheritance.

He switched his attention to the matter of dressing and getting some lunch. He was nearly ready to go down when the quiet tap came at the door.

'Yes,' he called. Nothing happened and then the tapping came again. Vexed, he flung open the door to find Dorcas, her eyes popping with excitement.

'Your father's home,' she hissed urgently. 'He wants to see you in his study right away. He's awful angry,' she ended with relish.

Martin stared uneasily at the girl's eager, snub-nosed face as his mind worked, hastily examining and dismissing possibilities, likely reasons for this summons. It was always helpful to have a line of defence ready prepared if possible. It couldn't be his recent loser on the steeplechase, for they had already discussed that one, and hadn't he been the soul of discretion about replacing whatever he drank?

'What did he say? Why does he want

me?' The question was hesitant.

'How should I know? All I can say is I bet you're for it.'

She glanced up at him slyly, speculating on the nature of his offence. Ever since her brief fling with him Dorcas had felt somewhat of a privileged person and permitted herself a degree of familiarity with Martin that she would never consider with anyone else in the family.

He pushed past her and headed down the stairs, in no great hurry to face whatever music was waiting for him. It was not at all what he expected and it was far worse. None of his genuine transgressions were involved at all and by a dreadful irony he found himself taking the blame for someone else.

His mother and sister sat together on the study window seat; Celia resplendent in a dark red dress and a large, befeathered hat of pinks and beige, Hannah in her usual sober travelling costume. The older woman looked upset while Celia seemed disinterested in whatever family squabble had spoilt her homecoming. As far as possible she tried to avoid involvement in the feuds and strife of even her closest relatives, unless they were her own immediate business. Celia was a natural born onlooker and, whatever conclusions she drew about other people, she kept them firmly to herself.

Neil stood by the fireplace, fiddling nervously with his watch-chain, his gaze darting uneasily from one person to the next and lingering on no one. He couldn't bear the perpetual tension between his father and brother and he resented having to witness this latest and worst showdown.

Gordon Warbeck was enthroned behind his desk, which served him as a kind of judgement seat. He fixed his elder son with a sour stare and ignored his 'Good-morning'. A minute dragged past as the old man considered him.

Finally he said, 'I assume your desperation got the better of you although I'm surprised that even you would resort to something so pathetically obvious as this.'

Martin looked quite blank.

'Am I going to get an answer from you?

Do I have to wait while you think up a plausible excuse? As a rule you have one ready made.'

'What? I mean, what are you talking about? I don't know what it is you're asking me.' Martin's voice rose in alarm. 'Presumably I'm being accused of something but ...'

He looked helplessly towards his mother, who began to say something reassuring but was interrupted by the old man.

'Hannah! Keep quiet or leave us alone. I would prefer you to be silent and stay, but no one is to speak for him. He's very good at defending himself and I want to see just how he proposes to wriggle out of this one.'

Hannah sighed heavily and did as she was told.

Neil, embarrassed, cleared his throat. 'Martin, please, don't drag this out. We'll be here all day,' he said quietly.

'What?' Martin almost shrieked.

His father snorted. 'All right. If I must spell out what we already know. There is over one hundred and thirty pounds in cash missing from this drawer.' He tapped the top left-hand compartment of his desk.

'Are you accusing me ...'

'Yes.'

Martin tried to laugh. 'You must have mislaid it. This wouldn't be the first time ...'

'The lock has been picked. There is only one key to this drawer and I keep it with me all the time.'

'Well I don't know how to pick a bloody lock. That was one aspect of my education you neglected.'

'Furthermore,' went on the old man, 'I see the horse is missing.'

'Eh?' said Martin blankly. 'Whose horse? I saw Gil walking them round the yard not ten minutes ago.'

'You're being deliberately obtuse, Martin, and you know how little patience I have.'

The young man threw up his hands in a gesture of defeat. It seemed he had already been tried and condemned, without even knowing what for. Gordon, he thought, was enjoying this, savouring every minute of it.

'The silver horse, Martin. The Pegasus horse.'

'Oh.' The word dropped heavily in the silence. The winged horse was one of Gordon's most precious possessions. He had bought it in London during the early years of his success—initially as an investment, for it was expensive. As time went on it became to him, not a good luck charm—for he was never superstitious—but a symbol of his prosperity. A kind of personal emblem.

It was cast in silver, with wings delicately carved from mother-of-pearl, and, wherein lay the real value, two little oval emeralds formed the eyes. It was an enchanting thing, this prancing figure, just five inches high, caught in frisking movement. It was not especially old but the craftsmanship was superb and even Gordon, usually uninterested in pretty things, loved it.

'You are well aware,' continued his father, 'of my attachment for that statuette and equally aware, no doubt, of its value.'

'Gordon, please, he's our son. The whole idea is ludicrous.' Hannah could no longer keep quiet. 'Whatever he wanted, he would ask you for it.'

A tight, humourless smile crossed Gordon's face. 'Ask? Oh, indeed he does ask—all the time. On the last occasion however he didn't get what he wanted. You were there yourself, Hannah. As for being our son, I think Martin believes that his kinship entitles him to help himself to any piece of his father's property which takes his fancy.'

'But he only asked you for forty pounds, nothing like this,' pointed out his wife. 'What could he possibly want with all the rest?'

The puzzlement on Hannah's face began to irritate Gordon. There were times when her kindness hobbled her intelligence.

'He bets, Hannah. He loses money at the racetrack and I have already made it clear that I won't subsidise him any further.'

She shook her head and murmured something about judging too harshly.

A panicky voice in Martin's mind urged

him to explain about Rachel, for he had no doubt that she was responsible. But that would simply mean replacing one offence with another. He had no wish to see his father confront Rachel Shea. She wouldn't think twice before telling him about their meetings, about the brat ...

'We've been burgled, that's all. Why don't you call the police?' Martin managed to keep his voice even.

'Yes, we could have been burgled,' admitted the old man. 'I note that the conservatory window is open and Dorcas says that it must have been so all night. But you will observe that most of the silver and glassware is untouched. It's hardly likely that a professional thief would leave behind anything so tempting. No, it is my opinion that you have a heavy debt and have taken just enough to cover it.'

Martin spluttered, groping in vain for some concrete means of squashing the accusation.

'I did not. I bloody well did not!' He slammed his hands down on the desk and glared into Gordon's face. 'You must think I'm simple or something. If you knew me like you think you do you'd realise that I'm capable of rather more subtlety than this. I don't advertise my so-called misdemeanours in letters of red. I'm a little more careful.' He stopped, aware that he was close to blurting out things that Gordon shouldn't know.

'Desperation,' said the old man, 'brings out the best or the worst in people.'

It was all as clear as daylight to Gordon Warbeck. He trusted Martin less than the servants. The boy was idle and frivolous and he spent money like water. When it was not given to him he took it. As simple as that. Unfortunately for Martin, the old man didn't believe in coincidence, and their argument the previous day sealed his verdict.

'I haven't touched anything in here,' Martin was saying, shaking his head in slow denial, 'nothing. And what about him? What makes you so sure it was me? How about the archangel Neil there? He knows the position in this house, he knows who gets blamed for everything.

I'm a gift-wrapped scapegoat, just because I don't plod off to some tiresome office every day like he does.'

'That's enough,' snapped Gordon. 'I've never had cause to question your brother's honesty and you are the last person with any right to do so.'

Martin scowled at his brother and then at the floor.

'Nothing more to say?' enquired Gordon.

'It seems pointless to say anything. You've made your mind up.'

'That's right. I have.' He paused for a moment, considering, then, 'I am prepared to forget the matter of the cash. I assume it is already spent and cannot be recouped. But, and I make no concessions on this point, the horse is to be returned by the end of the week or I cut you out of my will. Completely. Is that understood?'

The silence in the study was breathless. Neil and Hannah looked startled and even Celia raised an eyebrow in surprise. Gordon had reached the end of his patience and had nothing more to say. The loss of the horse had upset him more than he cared to show, doubly so because he was convinced that Martin knew how precious it was to him.

He got stiffly to his feet and left the room without a backward glance at his son's stricken face. As he made his way upstairs he heard the babble of argument and advice begin in the study. They expected him to cool down, see reason, retract his threat. Well, they were mistaken. He never delivered ultimatums in jest and Martin had better take this one very seriously.

SIX

Rowan Water was full of trout and had its quota of regular poachers, one of whom was Rachel Shea. A few hours at the north end usually produced four or even five decent sized fish—a good supper that cost nothing. Not that she needed to be concerned about money. Not any more. There was plenty of money now, more than she had ever seen in her life before. The excitement of handling more than a hundred pounds—a fortune—had dismissed from her mind the fear of repercussions. The elation obliterated everything else and anyway he couldn't prove anything, could he? Martin couldn't tell on her without getting himself into trouble with his father and she knew how he wanted to avoid that. The possibility that Martin himself would get the blame just didn't occur to her.

Had she known of this development and

his furious, frightened state of mind she might have thought twice before going to Rowan Water alone that day.

The fish weren't biting. Her handline floated motionless in the water, save for a very occasional dip and bob, when she hoped for an instant that there might be something on the hook.

Such a quiet, windless day, hardly a rustle between the leaves. Late afternoon passed into evening as she sat there, lost in plans and visions of silk dresses, scented soap and a house with separate bedrooms. The sunlight turned darker gold, the special rich light of seven o'clock evening sun, and patches of shadow in the woods behind melded together into pockets of deeper dark. Nearly an hour passed and the sun was reddening, its glare subdued into a clearly outlined crimson orb, reflected as a rosy pathway across Rowan Water.

The girl reeled in her line. She was rarely so unlucky. It would have to be rabbit again. Pity, but never mind. Tomorrow was Clancy Fair in Meadstock. She could go and buy, oh, anything, just anything she fancied. There would be stalls selling furmenty and lardy cake, toys, balloons—and sugar mice for Alec. There would be pedlars and tumblers, a hurdy-gurdy man, quack doctors selling 'miracle remedies', and maybe a Punch and Judy Show, not to mention the brightly dressed gypsies who always came to the fair selling dried lavender, baskets and pegs. With any luck there would also be a greasy pole contest, to win a plump goose or a sucking-pig. This time she could do more than look, this time she could afford to buy. Rachel hugged herself with delight. This was worth all the risk—in fact it was sweeter for it—and a thick ear from Cassie was a small price to pay.

The old woman had taken the money out and buried it somewhere until she had got everything together, ready to leave the district. She was convinced they were all destined for prison, or worse, and Rachel had finally agreed that it might be a good idea to move on in a week or two—especially if they went somewhere glamorous, like London.

Getting to her feet, she bent to pick up her shawl and—stopped, eyes wide, ears keened to catch it again. A small sound of movement. Not the wind, for there was none. It was more like the firm brushing aside of bushes, feet tearing through bramble and creeper. She straightened up and whipped swiftly round. There was no one there. Only pools of shade under the trees. A forest is a sombre place at dusk and she began to wish she had gone home earlier.

Drawing the shawl tight around her shoulders, she stepped through the shrubbery edging the water, and onto the path. It was stony here, overgrown. She had to pick her way carefully. About twenty yards further on her foot caught in an ivy creeper and she pitched forward onto the damp ground. Rachel swore and turned to get up, then her breath drew in sharply with shock, for the dark figure of a man stood over her without any word or gesture to help her up.

'Who's that?' The words came haltingly and for a moment there was no answer.

Then, 'You may well ask.' The familiarity of Martin's voice was not comforting.

'I ... How long have you been there?'

'Oh, I've been watching you for quite a while. I see today's poaching has been disappointing. Not like last night at all, is it?'

Rachel scrambled to her feet and feigned innocence.

'I enjoyed last night.' She tried to sound casual. 'You're the best man for miles around.'

'Tried them all, have you?'

'Stupid, Rachel,' she thought, 'you asked for that.'

'You know what I mean. There's nobody else I'd go with.'

'Never mind the pleasantries, Rachel. I want it back. All of it.'

'All of what? I don't know why you're so angry, I'm sure. You didn't give me anything last night. Well,' she giggled, 'nothing but a bit of fun.'

'You're wasting my time, Rachel.'

'Well if you don't make yourself clear ...'

She yelped suddenly as he stepped forward and grasped her by her hair, twisting a handful of it, jerking her face towards him. The girl's mouth thinned into a tight line of defiance. The money was hers now. Due payment. And the new life it could bring was too bright and precious to let go.

'I want my property.'

'Your what?'

'The money and the horse.'

'Horse?' Her surprise sounded almost genuine. 'There was no horse ...' She stopped, cursing her own carelessness. That was as good as admitting something.

'You really are a pitiful liar. You trip yourself the moment you open your mouth.' He slapped her smartly across the face. 'I want it back. Now.'

She didn't answer and he slapped her again.

'Go to hell! I don't know anything about any horse but I'm keeping that money. You owe it to me. If I can't have the money I don't care what you do.'

He thought about it for a moment, then,

'You can have the money,' he said sullenly, 'but I want that statuette and if you keep on stalling it will cost you your fine face and teeth, Rachel, and there'll be no more gents to take an interest in you, nor even those local louts you've been snubbing for so long.'

Her brain juggled feelings of alarm and puzzlement. Keep the money? What statuette? Why was he suddenly offering her the money and what could she say to convince him she had never seen his stupid horse?

'I haven't seen it. God's truth. Never.'

He cuffed her but she went on, 'There was only the money, nothing else, unless he ...'

'Who?'

'Alec.'

'Who the hell is Alec?'

'My brother. It was him who got into your father's study. I opened the window for him. But all he brought home was the money.' She hesitated. 'I suppose he might ...'

'What?' snapped Warbeck.

'He might have kept it for himself. As a toy. He's never had a real toy.'

'That toy is pure silver and worth more than your paltry hundred pounds. Now listen. You are going to tackle your little brother and relieve him of his toy before tomorrow afternoon. I'll be round to your cottage to get it.'

Rachel sensed a reprieve and curiosity took over.

'What is it that makes you offer to let me keep the money if I return this ornament, eh? It's not often I see you so anxious about anything.'

Martin scowled harder but didn't answer.

'It strikes me that something's worrying you in a bad way about that horse,' she went on. 'What is it, eh?'

His hands slipped around her neck, light thumb pressure on the windpipe.

'My father,' he growled, 'is blaming me for what you've done. And if that ornament is not returned he's going to disinherit me. Now I have no intention of paying such a price for spending a night with you and I will do whatever is necessary to get it back, if I have to beat the hell out of you and your thieving relatives.'

'You? He thinks it was you? My God, how he must dislike you!' Her laughter welled up with an elation that couldn't be checked. 'No wonder you're sweating. And if I don't help you you'll end up poorer and more useless than any farm yokel. What will you do, eh? Dig potatoes? Keep pigs? To think I could ruin such a grand person as yourself.'

She saw the whole thing as an enormous joke and, hoping to see him panic, she added, 'What if we've sold it?'

Martin swallowed hard.

'What if it's too late and the horse has gone? It won't help you to beat me or anybody else, will it? Well, it's my pleasure to tell you that we did sell it—this morning in Stennack. The gent was on his way to London and he never even asked where we got it. He gave me two hundred pounds. Just think, Martin, my love, I'm going to be richer than you from now on.'

Oh, this was fun. This was delicious, the cream on the cake.

'A moment ago you said you'd never seen the bloody thing.' His voice rose in consternation. 'You're lying. You haven't sold it. I don't believe ...' His words tailed off and he shook her, his fingers digging in, leaving red splotches on her arms and shoulders.

Rachel didn't care. She was enjoying herself. What a pleasure to see him squirm with anxiety.

'I have told you the odd lie in the past,' she admitted calmly, 'but not this time. There's no point in my telling you that I've still got the horse, because I haven't. I can't see any way of getting it back either, so you might as well know now.'

This time he believed her and the rage welled up in him like a red fog. Rachel had pushed her baiting just a little too far. It was her final and most appalling mistake for suddenly he spun her round and clamped his forearm across her throat, dragging her off the path and back towards the lake. The light was failing, the sky shot with bands of red and purple, as he hurled her down the bank and forward into the water, pitched in after her, waist-deep, ignoring her flailing arms and fists. His hands found the tangled mane of red hair and he held her under, watching the blurred white outline of her face, waiting with dreadful patience for the churning to stop.

He lost count of the minutes, had no idea how long it took, but as his reason returned and his grasp relaxed a sound—rustle and snap—broke the stillness. Martin turned sharply and saw, a few yards away at the top of the bank, the wide, frightened eyes of Rachel's brother. The boy was tensed, ready to run, his face shrivelled with fear. In his hand he carried two small rabbits which he had brought to show his sister.

The man lunged towards the bank, scrambling up the earthy slope in pursuit of Alec Shea, who turned and vanished at full pelt into the woods behind. It was now too dark in there to see very much. Each judged the other's position by the sound of his feet, crackling and swishing through thicket and fern. The boy found it easy to elude Warbeck, whose heavy tread announced his every move and pause, every change of direction. Within fifteen minutes Alec had lost him.

Martin leaned, panting, against an oak to consider the situation. What that boy had seen could get him hanged. If Alec went to the police ... But would he? How much faith did people like the Sheas have in the workings of official justice? More suspicion than faith, perhaps. Especially with the guilt they were nursing over the money. Prisons were hellhouses in those days, to be avoided at any cost, and he wondered if the Sheas would risk it.

Martin sank miserably to the ground, folding his arms over his head. It had all got so out of hand. If only he had caught that boy. Oh God, what a mess. He tried to clarify everything in his mind. Maybe, just possibly, the Sheas would say nothing, if only in order to hold onto the money. It was, he decided, a kind of stalemate and they were probably just as frightened as he was. All the same, he would have the advantage over them if he could get rid of Rachel's body—somewhere safe, inaccessible. He tried to form some coherent plan out of a welter of conflicting ideas as he stumbled back towards the lake to fetch his horse and haul the girl's sodden body out of the water. Somewhere along the way an idea emerged, a blessed solution, and he knew just what to do with her.

The Pinesetter shaft was estimated by some to be over four hundred and twenty fathoms deep. It yawned out of the ground on the high moors like some hungry throat and at least two people were known to have fallen in there since it was abandoned seventy years before. By law such deserted shafts were required to be made safe by the building of a fence or stone collar round the edge and while some of the mineowners complied willingly others were more casual about it and there were those who ignored the regulation completely. Whoever had owned Pinesetter had grudgingly erected a shaky post and wire fence—just measures enough to absolve him from blame if some careless person should take a plunge into that dank pit.

The hole was square and measured roughly eight feet on all sides—big enough to swallow horse and rider without much difficulty, so Martin had the sense to wait for the first glimmer of dawn, around 5.30 a.m., before venturing off the track in search of the shaft.

The desolation of the place was, under the circumstances, comforting. There were no early farm workers up here trudging off to begin another back-breaking day, no sound but the skreek of some predatory bird high in the air and a breath of morning wind.

He knew roughly where to find the shaft; a mile and a half to the east, across springy moss and heather. There were vipers out here, the coarse grass teemed with them in hot weather and he was thankful for his stout boots. The shaft lay in a hollow somewhere due south of the tor. He could remember the place from childhood, recall the awe and excitement as, gripping a post for support, he had peered down into sombre depths.

Coriander clopped patiently along behind him, draped with the still wet body of Rachel Shea. And then there it was. The posts jutting starkly out of the bracken, leaning crazily in all directions, with their links of wire broken and slack.

The sun was coming up, turning the sky from dusky to a fragile, milky blue as he heaved the girl off the horse. The body flopped down into the bracken and rolled onto its back.

Looking down at her face, he was jolted by the enormity of what he had done. It was not pity for her but fear for himself. This was how murder looked and felt. He recalled reading newspaper accounts of the wretches who were executed for actions such as this—faceless, unimportant people, so far removed from himself. Now, suddenly, he was on their level and his mind replayed the ghastly ritual—with him in the leading role.

But no. No, it would be all right. No one would find her. The shaft might even be flooded at the bottom—better still. He bent and began hauling her to the edge of the pit. With a grunt he pushed the body forward and it sagged for a moment, head downward over the wire, until the left-hand post, rotted by years of wet weather, simply snapped and, propelled by its own weight, the body rolled forward and disappeared into the hole.

He waited for some sound to indicate that it had hit bottom but none came.

A sense of relief followed gradually. It was all right. There was nothing to worry about now, except, yes, except the silver horse. There was no longer any hope of getting it back. Martin cursed violently under his breath. Damn her. God damn her.

He would have to get home right away. His clothes had dried off but he looked bedraggled, mud-stained, and Coriander was little better. Perhaps they would believe he'd had a fall. It was ten to six and he had four miles to go. With any luck he might even slip into the house without being seen.

Martin spent the next day in turmoil, waiting for the storm, continually expecting some emissary of the law to appear on the doorstep. He didn't want to stay in and he was almost afraid to go out. His mind had framed the notion that the whole world must know what he had done and there would be accusing fingers pointed at him from all sides. It seemed that his guilt must stand out all over him as if the word 'MURDERER' was emblazoned across his forehead. He paced from room to room and watched the clock, counting each moment as a step towards escape. Midday arrived. If the Sheas had reported him then surely the police would have been there by now? Every passing hour was evidence that the boy had not given him away—but how slowly the time dragged. He had had no sleep for over thirty hours and couldn't allow himself even a nap. To be awake was to be in control—if only partially. His dread was to wake and find three policemen and a hangman standing grimly round the bed.

His guilt sprang entirely from self-interest. Rachel was dead. That was Rachel's hard luck. The little bitch deserved it. Periodically Martin's fear gave way to anger. Blast her. She had no right to upset his life in this way and she placed far too much value on her favours. Martin hated uppity women.

Finally, when he realised how noticeable his mood must be, he took himself out for a ride to avoid prying questions from the family. It was fortunate that no one had noticed his absence during the night and he didn't want to push his luck. It seemed to Martin that he would never feel safe again. However at dinner that evening something cropped up in conversation to make him feel a good deal better.

'Gordon, I don't believe I told you, we discovered something very odd today,' Hannah Warbeck said, helping herself to more beef. 'About the Shea family.'

Martin all but dropped his knife and fork.

'No, dear.'

'Well, this afternoon Celia and I went into Meadstock and spent an hour or two at Clancy Fair. On the way back we took the opportunity of stopping at the Shea cottage. Celia admired my collar so much, I wanted Rachel to do a similar one for her.'

'And what is strange about that?'

'Well, she wasn't there. None of them were.' She gave a short, nervous laugh. 'And most of their belongings were gone—that is, everything that could be carried. They've just vanished and no one seems to know anything about them. It's quite uncanny.'

'I thought they liked it here,' added Celia, 'and fancy leaving on the day of the fair.'

'Well, they've not been very popular recently, because of Rachel getting herself ...'

'Neil!' cut in his father. 'Don't be coarse.'

'It's not coarse. I'm merely stating a fact.'

'A fact which will embarrass your sister.'

Celia smothered a chortle and shot her brother a reproving look. 'You're so indelicate,' she said loftily and Neil grinned. They had shared a quiet amusement at Gordon's prudery ever since the day Celia had expressed amazement that he could have brought himself to father children at all.

No one noticed that Martin had stopped eating and was taking in the conversation with close attention.

'She never gave me any indication that they were thinking of leaving,' continued Hannah, 'and in fact I find it all a little disturbing.'

Gordon shrugged. 'Perhaps they were in debt. It's not so unusual for people to disappear when they owe money. For such as them it could mean prison—eviction at the very least. You'll have to get your lace from Polly Hayes as you used to, I suppose.'

It was odd to hear them discussing the girl he had killed less than twenty-four hours earlier. Martin's mind sifted through the implications of this development and

118

found them generally favourable. It was far more comfortable for him to have the Sheas out of the way and he had been right, hadn't he? They had made the best of a bad job, taken the money and gone. His own lack of family loyalty led him to assume that others took their ties just as lightly and that the Sheas were willing to forget Rachel for the gain of so much cash. It was very convenient and moreover he might even suggest to his father that their departure was connected with the theft. It was no more than the truth—just less than the entire truth but it would have to wait until they were long gone.

He sighed and applied himself to his meal with better appetite. Maybe, after all, things would work out.

In a way things did work out, but not entirely to Martin's satisfaction. His suggestion that the Shea family had fled out of guilt implanted a morsel of doubt in Gordon's mind but not enough to make him absolve Martin completely. For several days he chewed the matter over, muttering about the benefit of the doubt, and finally worked out a compromise solution.

His will was amended, dividing the property equally between the three children. In normal circumstances and according the custom the elder boy would have the lion's share but Martin would now get no more than his brother or, outrageous insult, his sister.

Celia in particular was delighted and Martin accepted the decision with dull resignation. Things could have been worse.

Six years later Hannah died, drastically upsetting Martin's wedding plans. His marriage to the long-courted banker's daughter had to be postponed for almost a year and before their first anniversary rolled around Gordon too was gone. Two years later Martin and Helen had their first and only child, a daughter, christened Rosalie, in whom neither of them ever showed any interest. With every day and each event the memory of Rachel and her family became less of a threat and more of a curiosity to him, a kind of black puzzle to be revived and considered from time to time.

PART TWO—EARLY MAY, 1903

SEVEN

Where did they go? The question bothered him at odd moments when his mind was left unoccupied by the more immediate problems and pleasures of everyday life. And why, from time to time, did he feel compelled to come here? It was as if the place itself could allay the uncertainty, affirm that the thing was over and done with, buried and sealed in years that were gone. If only his memory wasn't so sharp and his imagination would not trace her features so clearly there in Rowan Water.

He was forty-five now, heavier and far less agile than he had been in those days, and his features had coarsened a little with middle age. He had become—certainly not mellowed—but perhaps to some degree disciplined by life, more cautious and discreet in his dealings with people. The Rachel worry was a recurring nuisance, like malaria. He had attacks now and then, when his resistance was down. It was not guilt, this feeling, but something like the concern felt on going out and later wondering if one forgot to turn off the gas, the kind of obsession which checks and rechecks and still feels no absolute assurance that all is well. Martin reminded himself that nearly twenty years had passed and that time, more than distance, was the best buffer between oneself and an unpleasant event.

It was early May of 1903, around five in the afternoon, at the start of what was to be a long, sizzling summer. Warbeck turned and headed for home. As a rule they ate at seven and he liked to take a bath first. Perhaps once or twice a week the family ate dinner alone but more often than not there were one or two guests, usually at Helen's invitation.

Her wide circle of acquaintances was Helen's raison d'être. She loved to entertain and her vast wardrobe was chosen to impress, please or intimidate these visitors, depending on who they were. On the whole the intimidation was directed at certain female 'friends', for Helen's clothes were always colourful, becoming and obscenely expensive. Fashion to these women was a competitive matter and, although it was generally agreed that Helen Warbeck was an intensely stupid woman in many ways, no one could fault her on her taste. She busied her thoughts with silk and lace, muslin and brocade—draperies both for herself and the house. Much of Hannah's simple linen had been replaced by more subtly expensive stuff and if Helen's conversation was tedious then at least her home and her person were sufficiently striking to excuse it.

She was small and blond, with a preference for rose pink, lilac and—the favourite—midnight blue velvet. By candle-light her blue eyes and permanently surprised expression looked less vacant than appealing, and her admirers were many. Helen was in her element in an age when intelligence was still a flaw in a woman and well-bred stupidity prized by the average man. They found it restful that she never made a shrewd observation or posed a question they couldn't answer.

Martin had married her for two utterly unromantic reasons: she was a showpiece and a good financial connection. Gerald Strickland was a country banker and had found it most acceptable for his daughter to marry into a family as well-to-do as the Warbecks. Gordon had told him very little about his future son-in-law and, like almost everyone else, Gerald had formed a mistakenly rosy impression of Martin which lasted until Warbeck senior died.

The souring of Martin's relationship with his in-laws came within five years. When Gordon's estate was divided Celia promptly took her share, married a naval officer and moved to Southampton while Neil, now firmly wedded to the newspaper business, bought himself a modest house in Stennack to be near his work.

Mainly because he was the married son Martin got Forest Rift and the surrounding land. However his father left him very little ready cash and it lasted only three years. Some of it went to pay everyday household bills and he resented every penny of that, but by far the greater part went, as always, on clothes, drink and horse-racing. Gordon's death was like the removal of a leash and Martin pitched himself wholeheartedly into all the pleasures he had only nibbled at before. Inevitably though the day came when he could no longer pay the bills and he instinctively looked around for someone to borrow from.

At first the loans were informal and Gerald didn't mind. They were smallish sums which didn't even call for an IOU and he paid out without hesitation. But they got larger and more frequent and the time came when Gerald felt it necessary to get the details set out officially in writing. The lending didn't stop until he finally recognised that Martin had no means of repaying any of it and the disillusioned Gerald was no longer interested in any of his son-in-law's pleas—not even with Forest Rift as security. For Martin the situation was worse than desperate, for no one else would lend him anything either.

At last, when there were no options left, he reached an agreement—albeit a bitter one—with the now hostile Gerald.

It had occurred to Strickland that Martin was not above selling Forest Rift in order to get cash. In fact it might shortly become a necessity and thus deprive poor Helen of her beloved home, for she was extremely fond of the place. She had always wanted to live there, which was perhaps her main reason for marrying Martin. Helen would have a fit if he sold it to someone else and that, Gerald decided, could not be allowed, for he doted on his daughter. He thought it over carefully for some weeks before offering to buy the place outright. It seemed the easiest solution for everyone and Martin, seeing no alternative, agreed. Gerald deducted the amount of the loans from the price and left him the balance as ready cash. Any hopes Martin might have had that his father-in-law would sign the house over to Helen were quickly squashed. Gerald was not that stupid.

Martin was seldom really conscious of the fact that Forest Rift no longer belonged to him. He lived there rent-free and still thought of it as his own for several more years. For a long time Helen didn't seem to understand or care who owned what but Gerald often reflected bitterly that, rather than finding a husband to support his daughter, he had acquired another child and was obliged to support both of them. He was anxious to keep the family together for Rosalie's sake. She was his only grandchild and, feeling that a stable home was essential for her, Gerald paid the bills for Forest Rift and maintained an uneasy peace with his son-in-law.

It was only after ten years of married life, when the money from the house was gone and he was utterly bored with his wife, that Martin realised just how precarious his position had become, for he was dependent on Helen's father for everything and any breakup in his marriage could spell disaster. No agreements had ever officially been made for his security. He was aware that he remained at Forest Rift on sufferance and sensed that Gerald was always ready to kick him out, so he treated Helen well because it was expedient to do so. Gerald's goodwill—what remained of it—was a precious thing and not to be put at risk. Thus, even when Helen's obtuseness and whining irritated him most, he stifled the anger, kept smiling and tolerated the guests.

She was alone when he went in to dinner that night. Thank God for that, he thought. No damn' silly people to tell dull anecdotes and decorous jokes, no political platitudes, no society scandal.

She was wearing a deep wine-coloured dress—a figure-hugging velvet thing of flounces and satin bows, low cut to emphasise the graceful line of neck and shoulders. Her hairstyle, as usual, was a glossy fantasia of curls and padding, combs and ribbands, and had probably consumed two hours of her time with the help of the maid.

Like all the other meals and 'snacks' which punctuated their days, dinner was a sumptuous and lengthy affair.

'Katie called this afternoon,' she said, beginning her shrimp cocktail.

'Oh?'

'Well you know what tomorrow is, don't you?' She looked at him expectantly. Martin strove to recall some reason why tomorrow should be special and found none.

'No, dear. I'm afraid not.'

'Oh Martin! It's five years, isn't it?'

He glanced at her silly smile and felt exasperation rising.

'Helen, we've been married more than twelve years.'

'Oh!' She tittered. 'No, silly, not us. But you have guessed that it's an anniversary.'

'All right. Whose anniversary?'

'Peter's and Katie's of course.' Her smile dropped a little at his lack of reaction.

'So it is,' he agreed mildly and went back to his shrimp cocktail.

'Well naturally they're having a party at the inn, and we're invited.'

'We would be,' muttered Martin, without looking up.

'Well yes. He's my brother, after all. Of course we would be the first they'd invite. You are strange, Martin. Surely you want to go?' She was beginning to sound petulant.

He sighed. 'Of course. You'd better go into town tomorrow and get a suitable offering for a ... What anniversary is it?'

'Wooden,' supplied Helen with satisfaction. It was terribly important to know these things. Martin considered them trivial but she knew just how important they were—like folding napkins the right way at breakfast.

Peter Strickland was Helen's younger brother. A humorous, tolerant man of thirty-seven, he owned and ran an inn in Meadstock. It stood near the outskirts of town, adjacent to St Mark's. Outside, where the road forked, was a large grassy area, on which grew a solitary maple tree. For this reason the inn was known as the Maple House. It had five letting rooms and an off-licence attached, together with a popular skittle alley. The Maple was not the cheapest place in town and this served to filter out most of the rowdy element, who preferred the less expensive ale-houses.

Peter had married a plain little person named Katie Deale—a comfortable, common-sense woman with a flair for hospitality—and she had made the Maple a haven for harassed businessmen and hen-pecked village elders and for anglers to celebrate or commiserate after a day's fishing. The place had an amberness about it, an aura of warmth which sprang from the log-fire, reflected in the brasses and the copper-top counter and winked along the rows of bottles. With it went a glorious smell; that inviting pub bouquet of woodsmoke and polish, wine-soaked corks, frothing golden ale and the bite of strong whisky.

'What time do we have to be there? I shall be in Stennack most of the afternoon, so we can't get there before seven.'

'Oh, not until eight-thirty. There should be quite a crowd by then,' beamed his wife.

Martin nodded and a knowing smirk crossed his face. Helen loved to make an entrance, to see a roomful of people turn to watch her with stares of admiration.

She chirped on, 'I've had a dress made. It's plum-coloured silk. I was going to wear it to the Levermores' party next month but I can always have another one for that.'

Martin never questioned what his wife spent on clothes since all the money came from her father in the first place. This dependence on Gerald Strickland wounded no pride in Martin, for he was accustomed to being supported, but he was annoyed by the need to pander to Helen's whims and not upset her. He had no desire to attend this wretched party, because he didn't care a lot for Peter and Katie. Their personalities were so unlike his own that conversation was never easy, blemished with long silences and jarring clashes of opinion. All of this bypassed Helen completely, for she had no ear for subtle strife. Neither was she affected by the covert bitching which always took place between certain lady guests, for unless the insult was spelt out and delivered with all the impact of a broadside Helen would miss the point completely.

Pandy bustled in to remove the cocktail

dishes and serve their fish course. She was seventeen, with the same frizzy brown hair and snub nose as her mother, Dorcas, and the same bumptious manner. Dorcas was now installed as cook and ran an efficient kitchen which produced spectacular meals. She had gained thirty pounds in weight and a husband both shorter and lighter than herself. The man had a timorous, jumpy way with him, which Martin privately attributed to Dorcas's fleshly appetites.

Perhaps the party wouldn't be too bad, he thought. Perhaps the Willards had been invited, in which case he would quite enjoy it.

Cordelia Willard was Martin's latest mistress. Helen knew about Cordelia as she had known about all the others and was in no way annoyed. They provided outlets for Martin, which meant that he left her alone—a very agreeable state of affairs. Helen found his habits in bed repellent and didn't hesitate to say so. This was not entirely Martin's fault and, in all fairness, she might have reacted the same way with any man. Helen simply did not like sex or any other activity that ruffled either dignity or hairdo. Well, it didn't matter. He could usually find someone else to keep him amused. It was only on the occasions of their rare arguments that Helen used his tomcat activities as ammunition when all else was spent, and this, as they both knew, was mere ritual, for she didn't really care. Their bargain was all but platonic—she had Forest Rift and his name, he had her money.

It was good to be married, Helen thought. In fact it was necessary to maintain one's pride. Old maidhood was the worst possible failure and with Martin to escort her in public she could flirt to her heart's content without danger of serious involvement.

EIGHT

The party was going well. Katie surveyed her collection of guests with as much relief as satisfaction, for there's nothing worse than a party that falls flat. But tonight there was laughter, cork-popping, the chink of glasses. The room was vibrant with flirtation, gossip, bits of scandal and business intelligence confided between special friends. Women's faces registered coy conceit at male compliments, pleasurable shock over bits of spicy hearsay. Men drank copiously, backs were slapped and a few arthritic elders forgot their years in the excitement and made frisky advances to the ladies. The women were dressed to kill and the room blazed with a pot-pourri of gold satin, black lace, creamy brocade, silks of green and pink, clouds of frills and embroidery, all so much more spectacular against the crisp dark suits of the men.

They had demolished the buffet supper by nine o'clock and the little band was just beginning to liven its pace.

Helen, as usual, had several admiring men in tow, while her husband amused himself in conversation with another race-going man who claimed he had found a system for picking winners. Martin was not convinced and his attention began to wander. He had noticed a girl, standing alone at the buffet table. She seemed to be with no one in particular but had clearly noticed him and was showing a good deal of interest.

She was slight and dark, with a face that was not quite plain, thanks to alert, well-defined eyes and startling, arched brows. There was wit and intelligence behind that face but for the moment she was obviously bored. Martin decided to investigate. There was no Cordelia to keep him amused that evening and just about every other attractive woman in the room had a husband hovering dourly nearby.

Katie disappeared into the kitchen to fetch the reserve bowl of punch and Martin followed her, angling for an introduction to the girl.

'Have I congratulated you yet? Five blissful years, eh?' He used the bantering tone which served for all women except his wife.

Katie turned with a start, almost dropping the punch, and glanced at the tall figure leaning in the doorway. She didn't actually dislike Martin but she would never go out of her way to seek his company—nor he hers. Fortunately for everyone, Katie Strickland was not Martin's type. He liked his women eyecatching and elegant and Kate was simply cosy. Dimpled and bright-eyed, she would grow rotund in middle age.

'You have actually, but thank you again.'

'My pleasure. Wonderful thing, matrimony.'

Katie ignored that. 'I hope you're not bored,' she went on, 'we did invite Cordelia but ... oh, I'm sorry. That was tactless.'

'Common knowledge,' he said lightly. 'I, uh, thought you might introduce me to the young lady standing on her own over there. The one in blue.'

Katie cast him a knowing sidelong look. 'Ah,' she said softly, 'yes, I see.'

'It would be rude of us to leave her there without anyone to talk to, don't you think?'

Katie laughed. 'Bring the punch then and I'll introduce you.'

Martin picked up the bowl and carried it out to the buffet table where several people were loitering expectantly, waiting for fresh supplies. The girl hadn't moved but stood surveying the noisy crowd, her glass of punch still untouched.

'Laurel, this is Mr Warbeck. He's my husband's brother-in-law. And Martin, this is Mrs Jay, who's currently staying with us.'

The young woman smiled. 'Well, Mr Warbeck, I've heard Katie mention you many times.'

'Oh?' He shot a doubtful look at Kate, who promptly excused herself and hurried off with a tray of crackers. 'And what did she say?'

'Oh, just that you have a large house in

a rather lovely setting.'

'Ah, yes. Well, it is very attractive, if I do say it myself.' He paused. 'And where is Mr Jay?'

'My husband died of enteric in the Boer War,' she replied gravely. 'We were only married for three months.'

'Oh, I'm uh, so sorry. It never occurred to me ...'

'That I might be a merry widow?' She didn't seem unduly upset about her late husband. Martin couldn't quite figure out how old she was—twenty-five perhaps. Certainly young enough to find at least one more husband. He wondered if she was also a rich widow. Her dress looked moderately expensive but it certainly wasn't a lavish concoction like Helen's.

'I suppose you're visiting friends in the area?'

'No, I came for the landscape. I'm an artist, you see. In fact that was how the subject of your house came up. Katie seems to think it would make a fine picture.'

If she was angling for an invitation,

Martin was only too willing to comply.

'Well you're very welcome to call on us at any time,' he said brightly. 'I'll be pleased to show you round and suggest a few interesting views. Very pleasant hobby, painting, though I'm afraid I've never been gifted that way myself.'

'You misunderstand me. It's not a hobby.' She took a sip of punch and helped herself to a crab sandwich.

'You mean you make a living at it?'

Martin was intrigued. It was unusual for a woman of any standing to work at all and when necessity forced them to it they generally ended up as governesses, although an intrepid few were now turning to the new-fangled jobs as typists and telephone operators. A female artist was a novelty to him. It meant of course that the late Mr Jay had not left her a fortune—or even enough to live on.

'Rather an uncertain source of income, isn't it?'

'Yes, but I enjoy it and I do have a widow's pension from the army.'

'What else do you enjoy?' he asked,

142

leaning confidentially down to her. If he had summed her up correctly she was not the sort to take offence at a gentle proposition.

'Oh, I'm quite a hedonist,' she said lightly. 'Would you mind fetching me another glass of punch?'

'What? Oh, yes, all right.'

He was a bit put out at being sent on this errand, just when he was working round to something interesting. It was obviously a diversionary tactic for he'd never seen a drink disappear so fast. He returned with the punch and suddenly Helen was at his elbow, flushed with flattery, cherry brandy and a set of murderous corsets.

'Katie's been telling me about your paintings, Miss ...' She faltered, looking vacant as the name eluded her.

'Silly bitch,' thought Martin. 'Mrs Jay,' he said pleasantly.

'Oh, yes.' Helen let fly with a piercing giggle. 'Aren't I a ninny?'

Martin gritted his teeth and said nothing. Helen was as high as a kite and behaving like an idiot. The girl however seemed to be amused with her. She listened to the torrent of inane chatter, smiling in the right places and nodding when appropriate. Helen was obviously very taken with her. She considered anything 'arty' to be terribly smart and had a private belief that if one surrounded oneself with such people some of the glitter might eventually rub off on one. Having no inner resources of her own, she required a constant stream of houseguests to keep her amused. The position was currently vacant and Helen felt she had found the ideal person to fill it.

'How long do you plan to stay with Katie?' she bubbled.

'Just until I can find cheaper lodgings. I want to spend the summer in this area. The colours are wonderful here and the place is so unspoilt. There's endless scope for the kind of paintings which I most enjoy but I really can't afford to stay at the Maple House for very much longer.'

Helen looked startled, but pleased. Strange creature! One didn't admit that one couldn't afford things, did one? But then the odd behaviour was all part of being 'arty', wasn't it? The opportunity was too good to miss and she pounced.

'You must stay with us!' Her voice rose with shrill excitement, so that several people turned to stare. 'We'd love that, wouldn't we, Martin?'

He was not averse to the idea. When Helen was out of the way they might take up their conversation where they left off.

'Love it,' he repeated with a smirk.

'You will come, won't you?' twittered Helen.

Laurel glanced at Martin, making a visible effort to keep her face straight.

'I wasn't hinting,' she told Helen gravely. 'I never impose ...'

'Oh, no! Lord, no,' cut in Helen hastily. 'I mean, we have guests all the time, don't we, Martin? I love to have people in, especially clever people. I think you're so interesting, and the lake is really beautiful, a perfect subject for you. I don't know what to do with myself at home all day long—I mean, one gets bored arranging flowers. Do say you will,' she ended pleadingly.

'You're very kind. Yes, I'd love to.'

Helen beamed triumphantly. 'Just wait till I tell Marcia Hart,' she babbled to Martin. 'She'll be furious.'

'God, she's tactless,' he thought with annoyance but Laurel smiled tolerantly.

'Now then, we'll send one of the boys to collect you in the morning,' continued Helen. 'I've got a lovely guest-room in mind for you. We're both ever so pleased, aren't we, dear?'

'Overwhelmed,' he answered humorously.

'I must tell Katie,' chirped his wife. 'Martin, Laurel's glass is empty again, get her a drink, go on.' She bustled off to tell Katie she'd purloined her paying guest, leaving Martin alone again with the girl.

'I hope you don't mind. She's quite, uh, forceful, your wife.'

He grunted. 'I wouldn't put it that way exactly, but no, I don't mind in the least. Do you want another one?' He indicated her empty glass.

'Not really.'

'Perhaps while you're with us you can teach me something about art.'

'Perhaps I can. We'll have to see what kind of talents you have.'

Peter Strickland suddenly appeared with a sombre-looking clerical type beside him, who had expressed a desire to dance with Laurel, and with a brief apology to Warbeck she obliged.

'Kate says you've invited her to Forest Rift,' said Peter curiously. He was a large man, with the brawny blondness of a Norwegian lumberjack.

'Well you know how Helen is, she loves to have guests. Mrs Jay didn't really get much chance to say no. How long has she been here anyway?'

'About a fortnight. Katie got quite friendly with her.'

'I imagine she'll be with us rather longer than that,' said Martin. 'Not that I mind, of course, she's very pleasant.'

'It's a good job you and Helen see eye to eye over these things, isn't it?'

Martin shot him a sour look for his

meaning was clear. Helen had to be humoured or she would throw a tantrum, and Martin couldn't afford trouble in his marriage. Peter half wished he hadn't said it. There was something about his brother-in-law which always tempted him to say these provoking things and he didn't altogether like himself for it.

'Excuse me, it's getting a bit hot in here.'

Martin stalked off and found himself a quiet corner out on the porch. His good humour had vanished with Peter's remark. A crate of empty bottles stood just inside the porch, ready for the dray in the morning, and, in a sudden flash of temper, Martin kicked it down the steps, wishing it was Peter Strickland.

NINE

The morning had been overcast, stifling, and the afternoon promised to be worse. She ran her finger absently under the close collar of her dress and wondered how to spend the time. Her first week at Forest Rift had been quite lively, for Helen had invited all her friends round to meet the fascinating Mrs Jay, who was an artist and whose poor husband had died bravely in the Boer War. Today there were no visitors and she didn't really feel like starting on a picture.

'Nothing to do?'

The girl turned sharply to see the man leaning casually in her bedroom doorway, then turned away again, watching through her window a group of wild ducks bobbing around on the lake.

'I thought I might go for a walk.'

'Looks as though we're in for a storm.'

'That's what makes it so sticky and oppressive indoors. A good storm would clear the air.' She moved across to her wardrobe and took out a light coat to carry, just in case. 'Where's Helen?'

'Gone out.'

Laurel eyed him suspiciously. 'I see.'

'Yes.' Martin strolled a few paces into the room and settled himself in the armchair. 'Gone to see one of her tiresome friends. She'll be away for hours,' he added significantly.

'You must feel very neglected.'

'Not in the least.' He grinned. 'It's a relief to get away from her endless prattling.'

'Hardly a tactful thing to say to me. After all, I am her guest.'

'Oh, but you're my guest as well. I'm delighted to play host to someone so —pleasing.'

'I'm thrilled that you approve. Now you must excuse me.'

She made for the door but he got there first.

'You are, if I recall correctly, something

of a hedonist. And here we are with the house to ourselves, a cellarful of wine and a selection of double beds.' He was still smiling as he pushed the door closed and leaned his back against it, hands sunk in his pockets.

Laurel looked wary. 'Anything I said at that party was meant only in fun. I'm afraid I drank too much of Katie's punch.'

'Risky sort of joke, I feel.'

'You mean it's about to backfire on me?'

'Madam, what are you suggesting?' His grin had become a little strained and she could sense aggression beneath the banter. 'I think you owe your host a little more civility.'

'Get out of my way, please.'

'That's an order, is it? Outrage and orders all of a sudden. Such a change of tune.'

The girl glared up at him. 'Your behaviour is becoming very unpleasant.'

'Not without provocation.'

'You regard refusal as provocation?'

151

'I don't like being, shall we say, let down.'

'Let down!' exclaimed Laurel loudly. 'Good God, anyone would think I'd promised you an affair. You misunderstood me, Mr Warbeck. I would have thought a man of your age could distinguish pleasant small-talk from a genuine proposition.'

That touched Martin on the raw. 'My age?' he roared.

'Well,' she answered stiffly, 'you're far too old for me. I'm not twenty yet and you, I suppose, are approaching fifty? It is, I know, a distinguished age for a man, but hardly the blaze of youth.'

Martin stood speechless.

'Quite apart from that, I could hardly be so treacherous to your wife after her splendid hospitality. I have a sense of honour, you see.'

Martin snorted. 'You're as cold as she is. Are you sure your husband didn't die of frustration?'

'Cheap tactics,' responded Mrs Jay, 'very cheap. I'm disappointed to find that your charm evaporates so easily. It obviously doesn't go very deep.'

He pushed his face close to hers, his lips drawn back in what was nearly a snarl. 'You can start packing, Miss, because your welcome has just expired.'

'That is up to Helen.'

'This is my house!'

'Is it?' A look of triumph crossed her face. 'Is it really?'

Martin straightened up and turned pale. He hadn't realised that she knew about his situation. This, more than her rejection of him, was too humiliating. For a moment he stood, uncertain, desperate for something cutting to say, and when nothing suggested itself he turned, wrenching the door open, and flung out of the room. The girl swallowed hard and relaxed with a heavy sigh, relieved to be out of a nasty encounter unharmed and with dignity intact.

One thing was certain—she had made an enemy and from now on it would be wise to stay away from him. Above all, her door would be kept locked at night.

A sudden rumble from the sky and the pittering of raindrops cancelled any enthusiasm she had left for her walk. She chose a light romantic novel to pass the afternoon as the rain gathered into a hissing rush outside. Perhaps in their different ways both the storm and the argument had served to clear the air. Whatever other illusions Martin might nurse about her it was best that he knew from the start she would never be one of his conquests.

For Helen Mrs Jay was someone to talk at. Occasionally, when her hostess paused for breath, Laurel was able to slip in an opinion or a witticism which, if it sank in, would send Helen into gales of laughter. But mostly she listened, and there was a great deal to listen to, for Helen would tell her everything about everybody, regardless of how personal the information might be. They went shopping together, took country drives, played cards, drank quantities of cherry brandy and discussed the doings of other people.

Laurel had a room at the front of the house, overlooking Rowan Water, and the plants had been removed from one end of the conservatory to make room for her easels and canvases. As the weather grew warmer she spent more and more time out of doors. It was, after all, the view that she had come for and often she left the house before breakfast to spend all day in some choice spot, quietly sketching.

Martin bitterly resented her continued presence. She was onto a good thing, he told himself sourly. Free living, everything laid on in better style, no doubt, than she could afford. And all thanks to his idiot wife.

At times he felt thoroughly sorry for himself. The money, he thought illogically, had no right to run out. It should always have been there. It was too bad of reality to be so disagreeable. All the same, there was a bright side. Thank God for Cordelia. A real woman. She'd have the trousers off a man like greased lightning, give him hours of rumbustious pleasure and send him home weak but satisfied—which was just as well with a wife like Helen, who nearly always said no. It was precious little fun when she said yes. He might as well sleep with a wet sack, he thought, remembering how she had screeched on their wedding night and told him to 'Keep those gruesome things to yourself.'

Worse still, he was without doubt a little less attractive than he had been—a trifle paunchy, grizzled around the temples. It was a hard thing to accept.

These days it was Neil who got all the women, having shed his pimples and filled out a little. He had, some years earlier, shifted his interest from the editorial to display advertising and now held the post of Advertisement Manager on the Stennack Morning Mail.

Neil was generous and agreeable and a string of lady-friends had led eventually to his engagement to a doctor's daughter—the lovely Virginia. His moustache was luxuriant, his face had character and Virginia thought the world of him. He smoked imported cigars, which again upset Martin, for Helen made a fuss about the smell if he attempted to do the same.

It was a puzzle to many that Neil and his fiancée had reached their respective ages without marrying—he was now thirty-eight and Virginia thirty-one—but everyone conceded that they were a good match. Except Virginia's mother.

Chloe Levermore was both bitter and indignant that her daughter should think of marrying into a family who had made their money from trade, especially after declining the offer of a coldstream guard some years earlier. To Neil it didn't matter what Chloe thought of him and his family but she was the kind of person who loved to make trouble for those who displeased her.

TEN

Cordelia Willard sat silently watching her husband stuffing down his breakfast. She noted every grunt and snort of relish as he jammed sausages, toast and fried tomatoes into his prissy little mouth. Always the same. Every mealtime this orgiastic feeding. It had long since rendered him far too fat to be of any bother to her in bed, which was perhaps the only merciful thing about it. Cordelia was left free to pursue men who were more to her taste and she did so with enthusiasm.

Henry seemed to billow around in a cloud of fat. Somewhere inside was a mild and not especially bright man, whose only real vice was gluttony. Unfortunately, that one vice eclipsed all others by its sheer magnitude. Cordelia wouldn't have minded if he had been lustful, selfish or even a little dishonest, but this devotion to food, this was a nightmare.

It wasn't always so of course. Cordelia would never have married him in that condition. Oh dear, no. In their younger days, when Henry had been large but not conspicuously so, she had found him middling attractive. But he had snowballed with years of abandoned eating and Cordelia, knowing there was no medical reason for his size, felt no sympathy. What upset her most was that he didn't seem to care. There was no depression, no self-doubt, no question of a diet. Henry loved eating, therefore Henry would continue to eat.

He finished his bacon and eggs, rounded off with a plate of toast and jam, numerous muffins and a pint of sweet tea. Because of his appetite the Willards no longer received social invitations as a couple, for the practical reason that he was so expensive to feed.

Cordelia was happiest during the day-times. While he was occupied with his business—an ironmongers shop—she was generally free to amuse herself in town.

Most evenings however were spent in hopeless silence while Henry dozed off his dinner and she sat morosely with a book, sans friends, sans amusements, miserable. They didn't talk much at any time, especially at meals, when Henry had better things to do.

Perhaps, some day soon, his overloaded system would just seize up. It would be something sudden, she mused, watching him out of the corner of her eye and nibbling on her single slice of toast. The day would come when his body couldn't take another trifle, another cream puff, and he would suddenly stiffen in mid-chew, baby-blue eyes popping with surprise, and keel over, dead. That was Cordelia's fantasy. She replayed it at every meal and tried to feel guilty, without success.

Cordelia herself was passably attractive; dark and well-groomed, with regular features and 'come-get-me' eyes. Martin Warbeck was her spot of light relief and today was Friday. He always came into town on Friday mornings. Cordelia tapped a long fingernail thoughtfully against her teeth as Henry lumbered to his feet with the customary belch and sigh of satisfaction. He gave a long, rattling sniff and his wife cast a venomous eye at the massive back disappearing through the door. Henry always had catarrh. Everything about Henry was clogged.

The minute he was gone she got up and rushed upstairs, long skirts swishing. She had a new dress to wear, dark blue with black trim, very elegant. A good figure was not only an asset but a mercy in those days. Being naturally thin, Cordelia never had to endure the agony of boned corsets to get the right line under the closely fitted clothes—unlike Helen, who went through hell every morning and evening to get her sleek curves. It was one of the things Martin liked about Cordey. She wore none of the severe foundation garments he had seen on his wife.

An hour later Cordey was ready. Fully coiffed and smartly turned out, she surveyed herself in the mirror. Dressing was a high spot of her day for she loved clothes. Women's dresses were elegant, figure-hugging, and the hats dashing, feathered and brimmed. She smoothed a hand over the panel of black lace down the front of her skirt. It had cost something, this dress. All on Henry's account of course. Ladies like Cordelia didn't work. And it was the least he could do to atone for his appalling self. It seldom occurred to her to feel sorry for him, although he was generous to a fault.

She nodded at her reflection, satisfied with the effect, and pulled on her beige kid gloves. The dress was striking, dramatic even. Heads would turn and that was good.

Cander's Coffee Shop was the local information centre. Any little piece of intelligence, any choice bit of tattle usually found itself tossed from table to table at Cander's. The place had an air of smothered excitement. Whisper and gasp mingled with the clink of cups.

Cream cakes squelched in agony as eager mouths clamped and chewed, dispensing hearsay between each bite. The warm, roasty smell of coffee hung gently in the air and in every corner and alcove trollies of gateaux and pastries nestled seductively. Cander's popularity was immense and the place was always packed with people. Everyone came dressed up and here affairs were arranged or broken off—all in decorous whispers despite which nothing was secret from anyone. The moment an intrigue was smelled in Meadstock it would be investigated, reported, dissected and judged by the scandal squad, most of whom were female, although there was a small male element almost as bad.

Here Cordelia met Martin Warbeck. Gossip was not one of his vices for he belonged to the opposite faction—the doers whose deeds provided fodder for the nosy. The atmosphere of Cander's was therefore irritating to him but Cordelia liked it and he very much wanted to see her.

Eyes followed them as they entered.

Hands bearing doughnuts paused in mid-air, their owners momentarily distracted. There were bold stares and crafty glances. Cordelia didn't mind but Warbeck resented it.

'Morons,' he muttered, steering her to a corner table as far as possible from the mob. Cordey loved to have a good view of everyone but he sat with his back to them, facing the wall.

'Business in town today?' she asked.

'I have to see the saddler. Anyway it's good to get out of the house.'

'Still got your lady guest?' she enquired. 'It's been quite a while now, hasn't it?'

'Five weeks,' he agreed bitterly.

'Neil seems to like her. By all accounts she's rather nice. Attractive?' There was a wheedling note here. He caught it and started to laugh.

'You're not worried are you, Cordey? That I might desert you?'

She dismissed that with a throwaway flip of her hand.

'Well I don't see much of you as it is, so I hardly think desertion is an appropriate term. But if you did defect, of course, I should simply do likewise. Two of a kind, aren't we?'

'What kind is that?'

'Shifty,' said Cordelia wickedly, 'discontented and unpredictable.'

His memory tossed up a fleeting image of Rachel and he wondered if Cordey was capable of killing anyone. It was unlikely, he decided, but the thought prompted a question.

'How's Henry?'

'Gross. Lethargic. His customary condition.'

'Loathe him, don't you?'

'I have my regrets,' agreed Cordelia cautiously. It was never wise to give away too much.

Warbeck put down his coffee cup and leaned across to her, his mouth curved into a predatory grin. 'Wouldn't it be thrilling if he dropped down dead?'

Cordelia's grey eyes widened in alarm. It was said in the barest whisper but it shocked her like a strident announcement to the world of her innermost wishes.

'Martin!' she hissed, dropping her danish pastry and slopping coffee on the table. 'For God's sake!'

He sat back and considered her thoughtfully. 'What an excessive reaction to a mere joke.'

Cordelia fidgeted, darting sheepish looks at him. Patches of red were appearing on her cheeks.

'It's, well, it's bad taste.'

'You adore bad taste or you wouldn't be so fond of this place,' he mocked. 'Come on, Cordey, how do you really, truthfully feel about him?'

It was appalling to be so easily read and she wondered how many other people had the same insight. Surely the ill-will she harboured for Henry didn't show? No, it was as she herself had said. They were two of a kind and this was merely the recognition of like for like. After all, his own character was pretty murky and he hadn't made his remark in condemnation. Her poise regained, a slow smile lifted her face.

'I wish,' she said, retrieving the danish

pastry from her lap, 'that I was a rich widow.'

He nodded, pleased at the accuracy of his guess.

'Is he worth much?'

'Hmm.' Cordelia munched speculatively on the pastry. 'I imagine so. He never discusses it with me. In fact he seldom talks to me at all, except to ask what's for dinner.'

Martin poured himself more coffee. 'As you know,' he murmured, 'I'm not greatly fond of my wife. Our marriage has deteriorated steadily for years and now it's nothing more than an arrangement, mutually convenient.'

'Yes, such a shame,' agreed Cordey, watching him closely. 'What did you say happened to your money?'

'Fraudulent conversion,' replied Martin gravely. 'If you can't trust your own stockbrokers, well ...' He shrugged resignedly.

'Scandalous,' consoled Cordey, still studying him. Was it true? There were several conflicting stories about how he had lost his money and had to sell his house. They were not all as tear-jerking as Martin's version.

'I often wish I'd married you,' he said earnestly.

'So do I,' agreed Cordelia glumly, picturing Henry poised over a plate of treacle pudding.

Never before had he said such a thing, although the idea frequently crossed her own mind. Naturally she had always shrugged it off as impossible, knowing he was firmly welded to Helen's cash. Life had its priorities, they both had to be practical and Cordelia prided herself on her realism. All the same. his words raised a tingle of hope—that feeling that some cherished fantasy might, after all, be a little more than pie-in-the-sky, a little more reachable.

'I'm terribly flattered,' she said at length. 'Do you really mean it?'

'Of course.' he said solemnly, toying with the sugar spoon. 'It's a shame you're not free.'

'Neither are you,' countered Cordey,

'but perhaps one day she'll divorce you.'

Annoyance flicked across his face. 'If anyone divorces anyone I will divorce her,' he stated curtly.

'On what grounds? Infidelity?'

He snorted. 'Helen? She flirts with every man in the district but she wouldn't have the guts to sleep with any of them. And if she did there's not one would come back for a second dose. My wife is a bore in bed.'

Cordey noticed the satisfaction which went with his contempt. The reason was obvious. Helen might be a sexless sponge but she would never make a fool of him. His vanity demanded that she be attractive to all men and available to none. Interesting. Cordelia wondered what he would do if the unexpected happened and Helen revealed hidden depths.

'Perhaps you don't know her very well? One day your little wife might surprise you.'

'Never,' said Martin firmly. 'I know all there is to know about Helen and it's not much.'

'But ...'

'You must excuse me, I've got one or two pressing things to do,' he said, glancing at his pocket-watch and getting up. 'I'll, uh, see you on Wednesday afternoon, won't I?'

She grinned. 'Need you ask?'

It was not until he was out of the shop that she realised he had left her to pay the bill. Never mind. Their chat had been interesting. She wondered which of his priorities would win if Helen did have an affair. Cash or conceit? Would he turn a blind eye for the money's sake or divorce her to soothe his pride? Cordey suspected a win on points for the cash—unless, of course, he had another rich woman to go to. Now there was a thought.

She pulled on her gloves, paid the waitress and left. On her way home she called in at the baker's and confectioner's for a quantity of sticky pastries, truffle and fudge. She had always known that Henry would eventually eat himself into his grave—well, perhaps she could speed the process. Let him eat. Let him gorge and stuff to his heart's content. He would die happy and she would be rid of him that much sooner.

ELEVEN

'Because they have no class, my dear,' droned Chloe Levermore. 'That is why I do not wish you to marry him. The whole family is ill-bred. I don't care how rich they are, but just look how they got it.' Her fat mouth quivered with distaste. 'A builder,' she muttered. 'Good God. Your father is distraught. I've never seen him so upset.'

Virginia was barely listening. This performance had been going on daily ever since she had announced her engagement to Neil Warbeck. It was tedious and pointless. Her mother's arguments were repeated almost verbatim each day at breakfast and sometimes dinner too. Ginny had long since ceased to argue. She simply switched off, knowing full well that her father was not distraught or even interested. Neither was he her ally. The doctor had opted out of the whole mêlée. All that concerned him was his work and after surgery he would shut himself in his little private lab for most of the day.

'You realise that waster at Forest Rift will be your brother-in-law? And you know, he's had a lot of women.' Here Chloe attempted a delicate little shudder. 'It's quite probable that Neil has similar habits.'

'Mother!' snapped Virginia. This was a new one and right below the belt. 'Your tactics sink lower every day.'

Chloe's pale eyes popped and her chins wobbled indignantly.

'He's turned you against your mother,' she moaned, crossing her arms over a vast and overbearing bosom. 'I who bore you and fed you.'

'Mother, have you any idea how tiresome all this is? When wheedling and whining fail, when bellowing and threats don't work, then we have slurs and innuendos. Really, Ma, you were only a governess yourself before you married father.'

Ginny got up to leave, unwilling to listen to any more.

'Virginia,' shrieked her mother, 'I'm sure I'm going to faint.'

'Again?'

'Oooh,' wailed the old woman, 'children bring nothing but misery. No gratitude, no love, just hurt and betrayal.'

'Feeling as you do, I assume you'll not be coming to the wedding, in which case I'll invite the Ormskirks.'

'Viper!' howled Chloe. The Ormskirks were close friends of Neil and she hated them. They were full of ideas—dangerous, radical ideas.

'I'm going out,' announced Virginia. 'I have things to discuss with the florist.'

Chloe sat and brooded. She was a hefty, humourless woman, alternately petulant and domineering. Her hairstyle sat on her head like a small, stiffly sculpted monument and most of her expensive clothes were too tight for the thick body inside. Each time he saw her Neil was reminded of a monstrous silkworm, ready to burst its cocoon. Strange that she should have a tall, lissom daughter with chestnut hair and delicate features.

Just a week to the wedding and there was nothing Chloe could do. Well, it would never have her blessing and if there was trouble to be made Chloe would make it. She reached into a little silver dish for a piece of cream fudge and sat chewing malevolently in the centre of her pink brocade sofa.

Chloe's house was designed to impress. Every lampshade and stick of furniture was draped and ruffled, embroidered and frilled with striped silk covers, fringes and a wealth of ornamental trash. It would never occur to Chloe that moderation might be the essence of good taste. She aimed to overwhelm and succeeded horribly.

Helplessness now engulfed her. Virginia always did as she pleased and Jeffrey refused even to stop her allowance. Chloe wedged another hunk of fudge into her mouth. It was a disgrace that Doctor Levermore's daughter should marry into what basically was a family of tradesmen. Chloe had never liked Gordon Warbeck. He didn't hunt or fish or indulge in any of the fashionable and respectable pursuits.

He had never taken his dutiful place on the local Board of Guardians either. Even Hannah declined to help with Chloe's charity work. Whatever kind of family were they? If the time ever came when she could upset that family in any way Chloe wouldn't hesitate.

Martin's horse came in last. Sourly he watched it dawdle past the finishing post, minus its rider. Neil looked sympathetically at his brother.

'What did you put on him?'

'Forty,' grunted Martin dismally. 'Arthritic bloody nag.'

'Oh never mind, dear. That's nothing,' chirruped Helen. 'It's all for fun, after all.'

'Is it?' He was feeling more and more surly. He never had a winner these days, was almost impossibly unlucky. Screwing up his betting slip, he stamped off to see what was likely in the next race. A youngish man who had been standing behind him strolled casually after Warbeck.

'Having an off day?'

Martin whirled round and scowled at him. 'That much is obvious.'

'Yes,' agreed the young man pleasantly, 'I'm afraid it is. Four losers in one day.'

'Do you want something?' Martin's tone was impatient, rude, but the other didn't seem to mind.

'Need a good tip?' he asked brightly. 'A sure thing?'

'They're all sure things till they lose.'

The young man produced a bundle of notes. 'I'm putting this on her.'

Martin's eyes flicked from the man to his money and back again. 'On who?'

'Darling Tansy.'

Warbeck thought for a moment. 'She's a real outsider,' he objected. 'Not a chance.'

'There'll be a good price if she wins—and reliable sources say she will.'

Martin began to turn away. 'I've lost enough today.'

'Well you know the old saying. May as well hang for a sheep as a lamb. Try a small stake.'

Warbeck surveyed him curiously. The man was about thirty and smartly dressed in a grey tailored suit. He had wavy hair and a face that was—Martin searched for the word—puckish, yes. He was about Warbeck's height and he stood patiently waiting for him to make up his mind.

'And why are you so eager to share your good fortune with me?'

'My good deed for the day. I've been a betting man myself for quite some years. I know what a run of bad luck feels like. Of course if you're doubtful it doesn't matter.'

He turned to walk away.

'Wait. You're, uh, on your way now to place this bet?'

'Right away. We've only got ten minutes.'

'All right. I'll try a small one.'

The young man held out his hand. 'My name is Conran.'

Martin shook hands with him. 'Warbeck. If she loses you buy me a large port.'

'Done.'

Darling Tansy didn't lose. She bounded home way ahead of the rest of the field, recouping Martin's losses and making a spot of profit on the day. He was jubilant.

Things would change now. The spell was broken. Buoyantly he took the young man along to introduce to his party, with the result that Helen promptly invited him to dinner that night. For once Martin was totally in accord, pleased to have found a race-going friend, especially one with contacts.

'Must we call you Mr Conran?' smarmed Helen coyly. She had taken an immediate fancy to him, although he was obviously a good deal younger than her.

'Michael,' he said engagingly. 'Can I call you Helen?'

'Of course,' she simpered, 'all my husband's friends do.'

Virginia watched with amusement, although Neil and Martin were unaware of the flirtation going on behind them. They were pressed against the rails waiting for the next batch of runners to come around the bend. Conran however seemed interested only in Helen. He stared ardently at her, regaled her with little jokes and offered her refreshments, while she fluttered and twittered, thrilled with all his attention.

As the horses thundered past no one noticed Conran bending to whisper something to Helen that sent her scarlet with pleased confusion. Martin wouldn't have worried if he had seen it for Helen's little banterings never came to anything. He would laugh at the thought that there might be an exception, a first time.

The sound of hooves faded. 'Did you have any money on that one?' Virginia asked Martin.

'No, but I may try the next. Any ideas, Conran?'

'What?' He whirled round, looking faintly guilty. 'Oh, well, let's trot along to the bookmaker's and we'll talk about it on the way. Only one more race on the card. Wouldn't do to miss it.'

'By the way, Mr Conran, where did you get that tip?' Virginia's throaty voice rang with curiosity.

'Michael, please call me Michael. It's quite simple. I know the jockey.'

'Ah, really,' she murmured, 'how very useful. But how can he be sure? I mean ...'

The young man's eyebrows shot up in a gesture of indifference.

'I've no idea. He knows about horses—which is more than I can say. He's passed me several winners this season, so I have a lot of faith in him.'

Beside him Martin's eyes lit up with the prospect of an endless supply of hot tips.

'What do you think of him?' Neil asked his fiancée as they watched Conran and Martin wander off through the crowd.

'Very attractive, very pleasant.'

'You know what I mean.'

'It's not unusual, I suppose, for a man to get a good tip.'

'He's struck up a very swift friendship with my brother.'

'I expect he likes company.' She laughed and dropped her voice a little. 'Especially Helen's.'

'Oh?'

'Oh yes. You've been missing it all. They were getting very close, very confidential.'

'You mean that's why he offered Martin a tip? To get acquainted with Helen?'

'Looks that way to me.'

'Where is she anyway?'

'Gone off to primp up a little, I think. I'll lay you a bet that the pink organdie dress comes out at dinner tonight. It's her favourite and she always wears it when there's a potential conquest around.'

'Cat,' laughed Neil.

'Not at all. I didn't mean anything unkind but it is her best dress and she keeps it for, shall we say, special people.'

'I hadn't noticed.'

'Men never do.'

At dinner that night Laurel Jay was all but forgotten. She sat quietly between Martin and Virginia, wearing a beige taffeta dress with a posy of pink roses pinned just below the shoulder, and made little contribution to the chat flying around the dinner table.

The main course that night was baked, sugared ham and cherry sauce. Dorcas was a great one for buttering vegetables and for squishy desserts covered with cream and brown sugar. Helen grew steadily pinker and noisier as she ate and drank and Martin, unusually good-tempered after a large win on the last race, even deigned to exchange one or two pleasantries with Laurel. The atmosphere was more relaxed than it had been for weeks and for a brief while the antagonism between Martin and Mrs Jay seemed to be forgotten.

'How is the painting going?' Virginia asked her.

'Oh, fairly well. I've completed four canvases. I had to scrap one or two though. Sometimes I get tired of a subject and can't finish it.'

'Will you show me your work sometime?'

'Certainly. After dinner if you like.'

'That would be lovely. I do so envy you. It must be wonderful to have a gift like yours.'

Laurel laughed. 'Now don't say that until you've seen my paintings. You might change your mind.'

'I doubt it.'

Virginia turned to Martin. 'Have you seen Laurel's pictures yet?'

'I haven't had the time.'

'He's always very busy,' Laurel informed her humorously. 'There are so many important things which claim a gentleman's time.'

Martin glared at the girl, detecting the note of sarcasm in her voice.

'Indeed there are,' he said acidly, his good mood vanishing.

Virginia fidgeted uneasily. She could see trouble taking shape.

'Some of them have hooves, others have fat husbands,' persisted Mrs Jay, taking a sip of her wine, 'but none of them require any unpleasant effort.'

Martin's colour began to rise. 'And what right have you to question my ...'

'Carnal pursuits,' finished Laurel softly.

In a flash he was on his feet, his face blotched with livid temper.

'You dare,' he snarled, 'at my table, in my house.'

The girl surveyed him for an instant, one eyebrow cocked in disdain.

'Merely a joke, Mr Warbeck.' She turned to Helen with a helpless little shake of her head. 'Really, Helen, you know how I hate to offend, even unwittingly. There was no rudeness intended. I'm so sorry.'

Helen, who had missed their little exchange, was irritated. She was having a good time and Martin had spoilt it. He stood quivering at the end of the table like a baited bull and just when Conran had been telling her how beautiful she looked.

'I see your good humour didn't last very long.' Her voice was petulant. 'Laurel is my guest. I'm sure she didn't mean anything rude. You're just being a snappish brute.'

Everyone cringed with embarrassment, except Mrs Jay, who gazed wide-eyed from one to the other and tried to look timid.

'I want her out,' he roared. 'She's been here long enough, the vicious bitch.'

'All I said was ...'

'It's all right, dear,' soothed Helen, 'he's had too much to drink, and the older he gets, the touchier. I haven't forgotten how you snapped at Anthea last week,' she said hotly to Martin. 'You've no right to be nasty to my friends. It's not for you to say who I should invite here and how long they'll stay.'

His features seemed to shrink, the

muscles drawn tight in a wave of humiliation. He hovered for a moment, fingers tightening on the stem of his wineglass, one hair's breadth from flinging the contents at his wife. Caution however got the better of him and he turned and stalked out of the room, slamming the door behind him. Laurel looked faintly disappointed.

Gradually talk resumed but the evening's happy atmosphere was gone. It was only nine fifteen but the party was over.

Virginia turned to Mrs Jay as she sat placidly peeling an orange.

'That was unnecessary,' she whispered.

Laurel bit into a juicy segment. 'He has no sense of humour.'

'I find your sense of humour distasteful.'

'Why? I didn't say anything we don't all know. There was no spite intended.'

'You were baiting him.'

'Nonsense. Anyone would think he was sensitive.'

'In some respects he is. Martin can't bear to be laughed at.'

'I wasn't laughing,' insisted Laurel. 'Lord knows, there's nothing very funny about him. All the same, I think it's sad when a man can't take a little harmless teasing.'

'Well I hope you won't do it again.'

Laurel's eyebrows shot up in surprise. 'My, how protective you are! Anyway, never mind him. Do you still want to see my paintings?'

'Thank you, no.' Virginia excused herself and bustled off to the library to cool down a little. A few minutes later Neil followed her and, having said their thanks to Helen, they decided to go home early. If Laurel had meant to break up the party she could not have done a more thorough job.

Conran however felt no obligation to leave and Helen didn't want him to go. They were left alone to flirt and chat and when he finally went home at midnight they had made arrangements to meet for lunch the following day at a very intimate little restaurant in Stennack.

TWELVE

'It's a Daimler,' said Michael proudly, 'a York Phaeton. I've had her for just over six months now. Six brake horsepower and pneumatic tyres. What do you think of her, eh?'

Helen goggled at the gleaming machine. 'It's, oh, it's just beautiful. I've never seen anything so elegant.'

She ran a delicate, gloved hand respectfully over the dark red polished bodywork and the great brass centre lamp. Both the back and front seats were comfortably padded and finished in shining red leather.

'She wasn't quite so smart when I first bought her. The previous owner had two awful kids and a St Bernard who ripped up the seating, so I had to fork out for new upholstery. She's not the latest model of course but I'm very attached to her.'

Helen walked slowly round the car,

fascinated, taking in every detail of this latest wonder. Motor transport had as yet made little impact on Meadstock and a horseless carriage was a rare sight. She had seen one or two of them in London a couple of years before, but nothing as impressive as this. She had often wished that Martin would get a car but he wasn't interested. He said they smelt and weren't a patch on a good horse. Helen reckoned petrol was preferable to horse-droppings, even if you couldn't spread it on your roses.

She was not alone in her admiration of the grand machine. Passers-by also stopped to stare. The men regarded Conran and the Phaeton with interest, while the women eyed Helen with a mixture of envy and suspicion. She enjoyed that.

'Do you want to come for a spin?' asked Michael. 'I could give you a lift home or we could go for a run over to Stennack and have tea.'

She hesitated. 'Well, I went to lunch with you yesterday. I don't want to start any rumours ...'

'A nice cream tea at Holly's?' wheedled Conran.

Helen's gaze lit on the envious Marcia Hart, watching sourly from across the street. Annoying Marcia was one of her great enjoyments in life and here was a classic opportunity—coupled with a genuine longing to take a ride in Conran's beautiful car.

'Yes, all right. After all, you are a friend of my husband. You won't go too fast now, will you?'

'Good Lord, no,' twinkled the young man.

With his help she clambered into the front seat and self-consciously produced a long, silky scarf to tie her hat on firmly against the coming burst of speed. With trembling fingers she grasped the edges of her seat as the engine puttered into life; the car swung out from the kerb and took off down the street at the breakneck speed of 12 m.p.h.

Fright gave way to delight as they left Meadstock behind and sped out into the country. An image of Marcia's glowering face lingered in Helen's mind and she began to giggle.

'Enjoying it?' yelled Conran, above the symphony of roars and rattles.

'Ooh, yes! It's fabulous. Can you go any faster?'

The car zoomed up to 20 m.p.h. She gave a shriek of excitement and clung to his arm as they swung around a bend and forked right onto the Stennack road.

'We'll be there in fifteen minutes,' shouted Conran. 'Not feeling sick or anything?'

'Of course not!' came the indignant answer.

'They do say I'm quite a good driver.'

'Marvellous,' enthused Helen. 'I think you're ever so ...' she searched for a word, 'progressive. You know, forward-looking.'

'I'll be getting a faster one next year of course. As far as I can see, the sky's the limit where speed is concerned. Cars will just go on improving year after year.'

Helen turned admiring eyes on him. 'Do you understand all about cars then? How they work and so on?'

'Quite a bit. I take her apart and put her back together every now and then, just to make sure she's in good health.'

Helen sighed happily and decided that this one must have even more brains than Martin. Him and his rotten horses.

They caused just as much of a stir in Stennack as they had in Meadstock. Conscious of staring onlookers, Helen got grandly out of the car and allowed him to squire her into Holly's for a sumptuous tea.

'My, it does give you an appetite,' she declared, forgetting propriety and attacking her cream scones with honest relish.

'Motoring, you mean.'

'What else?'

He grinned.

Helen blushed. 'Don't be wicked.'

'Madam!' he exclaimed theatrically. 'Can I help it if your beauty brings out the beast in me?'

Helen's peal of laughter brought disapproving glances from the other customers. 'I don't think you're in the least bit beastly.'

'You've never really had a chance to find out.'

She eyed him warily across the crisp expanse of blue cotton tablecloth, genteelly set with tea for two. What was he getting at? Helen was used to flirtation and innuendo, adept at parrying serious advances. Disturbingly, she was not too sure that she wanted to squash this one. Lost for an answer, she changed the subject.

'I hear you'll be at the wedding on Saturday?'

'Yes. I don't know what to give them. Can you suggest something?'

'Wine-glasses,' said Helen decisively. 'Virginia loves good glassware. It's what I would have chosen if I hadn't already bought a silver tea service.'

He nodded. 'All right. Wine-glasses it is. Where is the service to be held?'

'Oh, St Mark's, of course. There's really nowhere else since none of us is Catholic. Martin and I were married there. It was so lovely. I had flame-coloured roses and some little green ferns in the bouquet.

Everyone said we were the handsomest couple in the county.'

'Are you very fond of him?' interrupted Conran.

Helen looked puzzled. 'Fond? Oh, I don't know about that. I used to be—before we were married—but now, well, it's different of course. I think all marriages get stale, don't you? Mama always told me that. She said you just end up sort of jogging along together and that's all you can expect. It's true too. I mean, Martin's not much fun any more. He hasn't made me laugh for years. Sometimes I'm sure he's not even listening to me.'

'Don't you care?'

Helen shrugged. 'I make the best of things.'

Michael nodded. 'Well, never mind Martin. Do you want some more sandwiches?'

'Oh, Lord, you must think I'm a real hound, polishing off all this food. No, really, I've had enough.'

'I don't think you're a hound. I like to see people enjoying themselves. You know, we could do this again sometime, if you like. It's up to you of course.'

For a moment she wondered what Martin would say but then enthusiasm got the better of her.

'Yes, I'd love to. After all, there's no reason why not. It's all quite harmless.'

'Perfectly.'

'Well, uh, do you think we ought to go now?'

Michael laughed. 'Looking forward to the ride home?'

'I can't wait.'

Helen cast an appraising eye over the array of fine hats among the congregation and decided that hers was by far the best. Cordelia, who might have outshone her, had not been invited. From beneath the broad brim of her stupendous hat Helen surveyed the assembled crowd while the vicar droned his way through a ceremony which she, as a veteran wedding guest, already knew by heart. Most of the men looked bored and awkward in starched collars and Sunday suits, while their womenfolk hearkened to the service with faces that registered varying degrees of reverence, nostalgia or cynicism. A large gap beside Doctor Levermore on the second pew attested Chloe's absence but no one seemed to mind very much, least of all Virginia.

It would be over soon. Helen slid a crafty look to her right, where Conran sat, across the aisle and next to an elderly Aunt Somebody from Wiltshire. She would have a chance to talk with him at the reception—something to which she had been looking forward for days.

Fifteen minutes passed before everyone trooped outside to pose for photographs. Helen fretted silently, glancing at the church clock and wondering why it was necessary to take so many wretched pictures.

It was ten to four when the party began arriving in scattered groups at the Maple House. Virginia had decided on a cold buffet and the minimum of speech-making. As stomachs filled and bottles emptied Helen edged her way through the crowd in search of Conran, eluding her usual admirers. She had no wish to get trapped by anyone boring while there was better game to be had. In the end though, it was Michael who found her.

'Must be over a hundred people here,' said a voice at her shoulder.

She gave a start and turned a dazzling smile on him.

'Oh, there you are. Yes, Neil and Ginny have a lot of friends.'

'I've been looking for you.'

'Really?' She sounded slightly breathless.

'Then I saw your hat hovering beneath this potted palm and thought that you were quite likely under it.'

Helen giggled. 'When you're as small as I am it's easy to get lost.'

'I'm surprised Martin doesn't take better care of you,' said Conran solemnly.

She peered into the noisy throng of guests. 'I don't even know where he is,' she answered carelessly, then turned a confiding blue stare up at Michael. 'I don't suppose he knows where I am either. After a few glasses of champagne I doubt he'll even care.'

'Foolish man.'

She chewed her lip and picked a stray hair off the collar of his dark suit. 'Crowds are very tiring, aren't they? I'd love to sit down but there don't seem to be any seats left ...'

'I think we can do better than that.'

This time she didn't blush, because it was just what she wanted to hear.

'Are you making an improper suggestion?'

'Yes.'

She darted a quick look round the room to see if anyone was watching. They were all busily munching and talking. Martin was nowhere in sight. This opportunity might not come again and perhaps the occasion itself had jolted an urge in her to live a little while she had the chance. Virginia's wedding was an echo of her own so many years before, her own transition from hopeful to humdrum. Virginia had a better chance with Neil. Helen knew that and a pang of envy made her eager to win something for herself on this day.

'Then I accept.'

Only Virginia, emerging from her changing room, where she had retreated for a moment's peace, saw them disappearing up the stairs to the second floor and heard the click of the back bedroom door.

THIRTEEN

The thing that Helen loved most about this, her first real affair, was the stealth—the scheming, the arrangements, the underhanded meetings and the lies, lies, lies. She ceased to regard love-making as a sweaty form of assault and began to look on it as a kind of devious luxury, not a marital chore but a forbidden treat. The element of risk lent a whole new dimension to it, coupled with the delightful knowledge that her husband would be mortified if he knew. Helen had never been very eager to get Martin's pants off but she had a healthy appetite for Michael Conran.

She bought countless hats and dresses and spent hours in the bath and before her mirror. Martin, in his caustic way thought she was simply trying to fight off middle age.

Sometimes she was amazed at her own

ingenuity. Helen, who had never done much thinking in her life, was suddenly obliged to concoct a fund of plausible lies and to maintain an appearance of dull normality in order to keep her secret and thus prolong the fun. It was all very taxing and of course it couldn't last for ever.

Inevitably, people began to notice that Mrs Warbeck and Mr Conran spent a lot of time together. Within two months Helen began to get careless. She was seen coming out of his room at the Hopper's Arms one rainy afternoon, looking thoroughly flushed and rumpled. Then there were visits to the theatre, regular car rides and, flagrantly, afternoon tea in Cander's together. Within weeks Michael and Helen became choice topic in the scandal stakes.

Before long the only two people unaware of the situation were Rosalie, too young to understand or care what Mama did, and of course Martin himself. Laurel was only too pleased to help with Helen's arrangements, advising her, lying for her, suggesting new ploys to keep Conran interested. Helen was grateful, for pleasures, like trouble, are better when shared and a good ally is invaluable at any time. Laurel seemed to derive an almost uncanny pleasure from the affair—more perhaps than Helen herself—and some people felt it would do Mrs Jay an awful lot of good if someone found a man for her. It was sad, they said, that she was confined to living through someone else.

By some odd chance Cordey was among the last to find out about Helen and she might have remained longer in the dark had it not been for an encounter with Chloe Levermore at Mrs Entwhistle's 'House of Hats.' It was Thursday afternoon and Cordelia was trying on an autumnal concoction of russet felt, trimmed with leaves and acorns, all skilfully wrought in satin and wax. As Cordey tilted and turned the hat at various angles Chloe's face loomed up in the mirror at her shoulder and regarded it doubtfully.

'I think it's a little gaudy, dear.'

Cordelia's face fell. Then, attributing the

remark to jealousy, she said, 'Not at all. It's youthful.'

'Precisely,' said Chloe triumphantly, then added, 'Your taste is so much more sophisticated, dear. You're known for it.'

Cordelia glanced from Chloe to the hat and slowly took it off. She had been on the point of buying it but perhaps it was a bit loud.

'How is he taking it?' asked Chloe suddenly, peering owlishly into Cordelia's face. 'Very upset?'

'I'm sorry, you've lost me. How is who taking what?'

'Your friend, of course.' Chloe screwed one eye up into a conspiratorial wink. 'You know, about his wife and that man.'

Cordey reached for another hat. 'Which friend?' she enquired, trying to affect indifference.

'Oh, you!' Chloe gurgled with mirth and elbowed her playfully in the ribs. 'You know who I mean. Don't pretend. I'm talking about Mr Warbeck of course. You needn't be shy with me, dear. After all, my little Virginia is married to his brother, so in a way it's all in the family.'

'Do you consider yourself to be part of the family then? The Warbeck family?'

'Well, certainly not, but ...' Chloe floundered for a moment. 'But there are certain connections between us, I suppose—in the eyes of the law,' she finished grudgingly, remembering how common the Warbecks were.

'You were saying something about his wife,' prodded Cordelia, discarding the hat and selecting another.

'Well surely you know?'

'What?'

'She's carrying on with that young man. The well-dressed one staying at the Hopper's Arms. You must have noticed him, he's very attractive.'

'Do you mean Mr Conran? I've met him once or twice.'

'That's him, that's the one,' bubbled Chloe excitedly. 'Isn't it dreadful? Poor Mr Warbeck.' She watched Cordelia's face for a reaction but there was none.

'I had no idea,' she said lightly.

'Do you mean Mr Warbeck doesn't know?'

'Apparently not.'

'Oh.' Chloe looked disappointed, then brightened. 'Well, he's sure to find out sooner or later, don't you think?'

'That will be a circus, won't it? If I get any advance news of the showdown I'll let you know so you don't miss anything.'

'Well there's no call ...' spluttered Chloe.

'I think I'll have this one.' Cordelia cut her off in mid-protest and swept off to pay for the chosen hat, a green, feathery affair.

Mouth pursed with anger, Chloe watched her go. Common woman, no better than the rest of that tribe. Chloe supposed that there was not much Cordelia could say about Helen Warbeck, being so much worse herself. The doctor's wife gathered her dignity and grabbed the autumnal hat. She had loved it at first sight and it would look far better on her than on that Willard woman. Triumphantly she waddled along to pay for it.

Cordelia walked home in a turmoil. It

would never do to let the likes of Chloe see how excited she was but the news sent a fever of delight from head to foot. Perhaps fate was working for her. Henry hadn't been very well lately—he wheezed a lot and once or twice he fell over. Brimming with concern, Cordey made clucking noises and soothed him with suet pudding and he felt he was well cared for. Never for a moment did he question his wife's motives. He thought the sudden wealth of cakes and pies which appeared on the table was designed to make him happy. Poor Henry.

One Tuesday morning in early September Henry Willard died in very much the way that Cordelia had always hoped he would. A seizure of some vital organ gripped him as he bent, puffing, to fetch a carton of nails from beneath his shop counter and within forty seconds Cordelia was a widow.

She displayed a lot of noisy public grief and camouflaged her glee superbly when informed that he had left her about

£60,000, which was a staggering sum for a mere shopkeeper. As soon as the burial uproar was over and the tearful relatives had gone home, full of sherry and cold cuts, Cordelia's mind turned to practical things. With so much cash she didn't actually need a man, not financially at any rate. Widowhood needn't necessarily be lonely, especially when one has money. All the same, she wasn't getting any younger and it might be nice to have one around.

Her first and obvious choice was Martin Warbeck and right at her fingertips lay the means to get him. Helen's affair. The charge was ready laid. All she had to do was light the fuse and stand clear. And so, one morning shortly after the funeral, Cordey sat down and addressed a brief note to Martin—an invitation to visit her at home. It was time, she thought, to get things moving.

FOURTEEN

'My poor Martin,' cooed Cordelia, pressing his head against her ample bust.

'What?' He was nearly asleep, worn out and satisfied.

'Poor dear,' she murmured again.

With some annoyance he opened one eye and peered up at her. 'Who's a poor dear? Why?'

Cordey didn't answer. She gazed down at him compassionately and gave a sorrowful shake of her head.

'What the hell is the matter with you?' He sat up, irritable and alarmed.

'Nothing,' she said pityingly, stroking his back, 'don't upset yourself.'

'Over what? For God's sake, woman ...'

'Perhaps you ought to know,' pondered Cordelia, 'but I don't think it's my place to say anything.'

'Cordelia, I'm going to lose my temper if you don't stop dropping these mournful hints.'

Cordey judged that he was just about ready. She looked him steadily in the eye. 'Your wife is having an affair.'

She wasn't surprised when he laughed. She was half expecting it.

'A serious one, Martin. A man called Conran. The whole damn town is talking about it.'

She watched the smile melt from his face, replaced by something uncertain—disbelief, suspicion.

'I hate to see people laughing at you,' she went on innocently, knowing that ridicule was one thing he could never stand. 'Why don't you ask your brother? Or Peter Strickland?'

She was serious. It wasn't one of her jokes. Martin thought back, searching for some occurrence, some remark that should have made him suspicious. Why was Helen always giggling? And what did that bitch Laurel look so pleased about these days? He remembered then the awkward silences with his in-laws and the abrupt change of subject whenever the conversation touched on his racing friend, Conran. And how often the man had called at Forest Rift when he was out. There was always a little note or card saying 'Sorry to have missed you.' Martin had never given it a second thought before.

Cordelia watched the effect of her words, watched the lines of his face draw down and his eyes turn that yellowish colour they always did when he was really angry. Suddenly he flung back the covers and made a lunge for his clothes. Cordey thought dryly that she had seen trousers ripped off but never seen anyone rip them on before. He tore out of the house with his clothing twisted, one boot unlaced, his hair uncombed.

Cordelia sat up in bed, tense with pleasure and fright. It had worked. She felt a tremor of anticipation and chewed on a thumbnail, eyes bright with excitement. Martin was as good as hers, she felt sure. It was just a matter of time.

Virginia heard Helen screaming long before the pony-trap pulled up to the front door. Not screams of fright, but rage—howling, hysterical temper, coming from the front parlour. There were one or two crashes and Martin's voice, lower but obviously angry.

Kerry, the driver, turned to Virginia and winked.

'Shall I take you back, Miss?'

'No, she's expecting me. Anyway I'm fraught with curiosity.'

She was already half convinced that Helen had finally been found out when Pandy opened the door, bubbling with details of the fight, which had been going on for at least half an hour.

'He knows about Mr Conran,' hissed the girl.

'Pandy ...'

'You should hear what Missus has been calling Mr Warbeck.'

'This is no business of yours.'

'And then he slapped her. Twice. I heard it—like a gunshot it was,' went on the maid, undeterred. 'When I took the tea-tray in she grabbed it from me and threw it at him. All the hot water went over his trousers ...'

'Pandy!'

'Sorry, miss.' The girl slunk reluctantly off to the kitchen, one ear still cocked for sounds of combat from the parlour.

Virginia knocked at the door but the soft tapping was drowned by the argument within:

'As far as I'm concerned it is my house. It's Papa's money that keeps it going. You're no more than a lodger here, so I'll invite who I please and see who I please.'

'You won't see him again, at home or anywhere else. I'm not having my wife make a bloody fool out of me.'

'And what about your woman, eh? What about that tawdry, middle-aged baggage at the ironmonger's shop?'

'She's a hell of a lot younger than you are,' bellowed Warbeck. 'You're forty, Helen. Forty and stupid and losing your figure. I'm damned sure it's not your scintillating conversation he's after. The only thing a young man would want from a moron like you is money.'

Outside, Virginia winced.

'If you died tomorrow.' screeched Helen, 'I can name a dozen men who would rush to marry me, and Michael would be first.'

'For money,' repeated Martin, ignoring the fact that this had been his own reason for marrying her. 'Just money.'

'He's a gentleman. You were never a gentleman. The awful things you wanted me to do in bed ...'

'Such delicacy,' sneered her husband. 'And he doesn't, I suppose?'

'You never had any finesse,' snapped Helen, 'pummelling me and squeezing me, poke, poke, poke. You're horrible.'

'I suppose he's found a better way?' snarled Martin.

'He's better than you are—and younger,' added his wife with satisfaction. 'I notice the younger women aren't so interested in you any more. Laurel, for instance.'

That really stung.

'I'll bet you're the most boring lay

he's ever had. Like a bloody chicken carcass. He's probably got some warm little tart tucked away somewhere to give him a bit of relief after a session with you.'

'You, Martin, are not very appetising in a state of undress. You have grown a paunch and things are beginning to sag, my dear. Is it surprising that I turn to a man with more bounce and rather less droop?'

'Oh my God!' whispered Virginia, clapping a hand to her mouth.

'The very sight of you is enough to turn a man impotent.' His voice was quivering. 'God, I wonder what he thought when he saw you without your face-paint and your stays.'

'He thinks I'm beautiful,' announced Helen triumphantly.

'You're an idiot!' roared Martin. 'And if he comes here again I'll kill him. Furthermore, you will not leave this house without me. If necessary I'll lock you in your damned bedroom indefinitely.'

'Do try,' came the defiant response. 'My

215

father would kick you out of here at one word from me.'

'Damn your bloody father.'

'Being a little reckless, aren't we? Who else would lend you money? Nobody would even give you work. You've been useless all your life,' snarled Helen.

Virginia, poised to tap a second time, was nearly knocked over as the door crashed open and Helen flew past her and up the stairs.

'Reptile!' she shrieked over her shoulder.

'Hag!' bellowed her husband in return.

Weeping and swearing, Helen disappeared round the bend at the top of the stairs and a door slammed. There was a scrabbling sound and a loud bang as the bolt shot home. The silence that followed was almost unnerving. Virginia peered round the door at Martin, standing flushed and furious amidst the wreckage of what had been a very smart parlour. Bits of glass and china littered the floor and furniture, Helen's rosewood sewing table leaned precariously with one leg snapped off and a fruit knife protruded from the sofa at the end of a long, vicious cut, from which the stuffing was beginning to ooze. Both Martin and the carpet were splattered with tea-stains.

'She did this,' he said sullenly, as Virginia's appalled eyes took in the damage. 'I never knew she was capable of such behaviour.'

Virginia didn't quite know what to say. It was obviously a mortal blow to his pride and, what was worse, instead of cowering in shame, Helen had fought back. He looked a bit lost. Ginny fidgeted, wishing she had taken Kerry's advice and gone home.

'I'll go if you like. I came to see Helen really but ...'

His eyes slowly lifted to meet hers. 'You knew about it,' he said resentfully, 'you and my self-satisfied bloody brother. Why didn't you tell me, eh? Enjoying it too much? You let it go on, everybody laughing at me, and never said a word.'

'Martin, I never interfere in other people's problems.'

'You're just as underhanded as she is.'

He took a few steps towards her and Virginia began to back away.

'I suppose you and Neil got a lot of satisfaction out of this, didn't you? He's jealous of me, always has been. Because he's a plodder, he's mediocre and boring.'

At that Virginia felt her temper give way.

'Your brother is well-liked and everything he has he's worked hard for. You're a sponger, Martin, and you've never respected anyone or contributed anything to this family. Maybe our Mr Conran does want Helen's money. Well, you should be able to understand that. What did you marry her for if not her money? And do you think she hasn't realised it? It may have taken her a few years but I think she's seen the light. On the other hand, it's not inconceivable that Michael is actually fond of her. You're very quick to graft your own motives onto somebody else, aren't you? I think it's quite understandable that she's found herself another man. And you're not entitled to all this outrage and self-pity, Martin, truly you're not. What's more, neither Neil nor I rely for entertainment on anything so sad and trivial as your domestic squabbles.'

Without warning Martin slapped her, hard, across the face. The marks of his fingers stood out in angry red against the pallor of her cheek.

'If you wanted to make an enemy of your brother,' she said coldly, 'you've just found the perfect way. This is the last time you'll see me or any of mine in this house. No matter what happens to you, Martin, we won't be there to help. And if you continue this way with Helen you're liable to end up ...'

'Good riddance.' He turned his back, glaring at Ginny's reflection in the mirror over the fireplace. He saw her leave and the door close behind her. That was just fine. He didn't want to see either of them again. What could they do for him anyway?

What indeed? Martin had made a bad mistake, for the time was to come when he would need friends.

When he finally went to bed that night more destruction awaited him. Every piece of clothing he possessed had been slashed, shredded almost, with a pair of dressmaking scissors, on which, as a symbolic gesture, Helen had impaled a pair of his britches, right through the crutch.

He raged across the landing to her bedroom and not surprisingly found the door locked. The only reply to his hammering and threats was a sharp burst of abuse from within, followed by stubborn silence.

He turned for solace to a bottle of port and stayed up till 2 a.m. to finish it. As he drank his thoughts turned to Cordelia. There were worse prospects than a rich widow. He need no longer rely on Helen at all. Cordey had always been keen on him and now that Henry was gone there was nothing to stand in their way—except Helen. It should be fairly easy to arrange a divorce, he thought happily. If the whole town was talking about Helen there would be no difficulty in proving her guilt. She would soon discover that a man could get away with his indiscretions but a woman could not.

FIFTEEN

It's always wise to be sure of one's ground before making a big decision and for this reason Martin called on Cordelia the following day to try out her attitude to possible marriage. She was, as he expected, enthusiastic.

'Of course!' Cordelia clapped her hands and threw her arms around his neck. 'How long will the divorce take?'

'I don't know much about such things but I'll make it as quick as possible.'

'I can't wait to tell everyone.'

'No! That wouldn't help at all. You're to keep quiet about it. People will say I'm simply divorcing her to marry you.'

'Well, aren't you?' said Cordey petulantly.

'Yes, but,' he hesitated, 'there's no need to make it stickier than it is. Divorces are never pleasant.'

223

'Would you marry me if I wasn't so rich?' demanded Cordey sharply.

'You know I would,' he answered, looking her in the eye.

'I don't think so,' rejoined Cordelia. 'Nevertheless we're both adults and I know that you have to be practical, so I won't hold it against you. Anyway I think we're well matched.'

She knew that her money was a decisive factor in this proposal. It took the icing off the cake of course but in middle age realism came first. Circumstances had conspired to make this possible and Lord knows she had wished for it often enough. It would be foolish to throw it all away over a bit of juvenile idealism. He would make a good mate for her and, most important, he had many contacts and acquaintances. If there was one thing Cordey was short of, it was friends and social life.

'When will you see your solicitor?'

'Unfortunately he's gone off on holiday for a week or two but I'll start the ball rolling as soon as he gets back.'

'Have you told Helen yet?'

'No, I'd like to see the solicitor and be sure of my ground before I do that but I don't foresee any difficulties now that she's made such an exhibition of herself.'

Cordelia beamed. 'I think we should celebrate. There's a bottle of Napoleon brandy in the cabinet.'

He poured large measures for them both. 'You did it on purpose, didn't you?' he said, handing her a glass.

'What?'

'Told me about Helen.'

'You would have found out sooner or later. I thought it might be less painful coming from me,' she said lightly, then crimsoned as he raised a sarcastic eyebrow.

'You wanted me to marry you,' he stated bluntly, 'don't try and dress it up.'

She swallowed her brandy in one gulp and held out her glass for a refill. 'All right, yes. You don't enjoy being married to her, do you? And you always said that if you were free ...'

'I'm not criticising. I think it's an excellent idea but let's be honest about it, eh?'

She settled back on the sofa. 'All right, there's nothing giddy or romantic about it but it suits both of us.'

Martin raised his glass. 'There you have it, my dear.'

'The first thing I shall do,' said Cordey thoughtfully, 'is sell that fusty old shop. All the cardboard boxes full of nails and washers, all the wire netting and the paraffin, and the tools, putty and paint.' Disgust crept into her voice.

He grinned. 'Not glamorous enough for you?'

'No, that's right. It's not. I want a shop like Mrs Entwhistle's or Polly Hayes's dress shop.'

'What do you know about running a business?'

Cordelia waved a hand vaguely. 'Oh, I'd get someone else to do that for me. I can afford it.'

'No doubt. And where would we live? I don't suppose you want to stay here?'

'I suppose we could move to Stennack. There are some quite nice houses on the outskirts.'

'Not much entertainment though,' suggested Martin slyly, 'and I think you're the sort of person to appreciate, say, London?'

The idea certainly appealed to her. Yes, think of all the theatres and music halls, all the wonderful shops.

'Oh Martin?' She was trembling with glee. 'It's all going to be marvellous. Have another brandy.'

There was nothing more to be done until the solicitor returned. After that the sordid, acrimonious process of divorce would begin. Two days had passed since their argument and Helen remained locked in her room, refusing to talk to anyone but Laurel. Martin had spent the morning out riding, he had read the papers and eaten his lunch and now found himself lost for something to do. Aimlessly he drifted out into the conservatory and there saw something that caught his interest.

It was the first time he had taken a good look at Laurel's pictures. There were now eight canvases arrayed at one end of the conservatory. She had never before left them uncovered and he was immediately intrigued by their dreamlike quality. Fantasy images, misty colours and forms which ranged from delicate to sombre. The places were real—he recognised most of them with no difficulty—but she had endowed them with a special atmosphere. What was it? A drowsy feeling of other-time, the not-quite-here-and-now. Not quite anytime. Or was it?

A comparison sprang to mind. It was like the painted scenery he had seen at the theatre long years before, when Hannah took them all to see 'A Midsummer Night's Dream.' The effect was similar—a backdrop for drama, for some wonder or tragedy. His eyes flicked uneasily from canvas to canvas. There was one of the lake at sunset, drawn from beneath the trees by the water's edge on a gentle summer evening, the sky bright with heather colours. Almost like ... But not quite the same. Not the exact spot.

And what about this one of the moor?

An empty picture, he thought, a vista of coarse brown grassland, featureless save for patches of bracken and a scattering of boulders. A cold picture without any focal point. Except—he frowned and leaned closer, squinting to see the little detail sketched at the bottom right-hand corner. It was very clear once you noticed it, that circle of wooden posts projecting from the bracken in dark silhouette against a milky sky.

Martin straightened up, troubled. He moved on to study the other paintings. Nothing strange about any of them, just views. Done in the same style of course but without any disquieting associations. He relaxed a little. It was coincidence. Lakes at sunset were almost de rigueur for an artist, he told himself, surveying the last canvas. He didn't recognise this one at all. It seemed to portray the badly lit interior of some labourer's dwelling, where a child sat, spooning gruel. A poor place, clean but spartan and of no interest to him. Mrs Jay displayed very odd taste ...

The crash came in a moment of shock

that almost stopped his heart. One instant seemed to draw itself out to trembling length as he whirled and ducked, arms flung up to protect his head. His breath drew violently in and released in a scream which blended with the sharp crack and tinkle of falling glass and the heavy smack of the slate as it hit the stone floor beside him and broke apart.

The sound died, his taut muscles relaxed into an all-over shake and his gaze swivelled from the slate up to the jagged hole punched in the glass roof. He shook his head and bits of glass dropped plinking to the floor. Trembling, he brushed his shoulders off and winced as tiny splinters burrowed under the skin. Just four or five inches to the right and that slate might have split his skull. He felt the nausea building inside him and was about to yell for the maid when she appeared round the corner and halted, goggle-eyed, her hand clapped to her mouth.

'Fetch Gil,' he snarled.

'Are you all right, sir?'

'I'm still standing, aren't I?'

'Well I suppose you are but your neck's bleeding something shocking.'

'What?' He looked to where she pointed at the spreading red stain on his shirt. There was a gash just above his collarbone and a splinter of glass about an inch long was embedded just beneath the skin.

'You'd better get Dorcas too.'

'She's doing the potroast ...'

'Are you arguing? Do you want me to bleed to death because she's too busy with the potroast? Go and get her,' he bellowed.

Terrified, the girl scuttled off and a few minutes later the odd-jobber presented himself. He surveyed Warbeck and the shattered roof without comment or sign of concern.

'Don't you ever check the roof?' Martin's voice shook with temper.

'Once a month,' said Gil shortly.

'Then you'd better make it once a week.' Martin pointed to the slate. 'Nearly bloody killed me. I suppose you just couldn't be bothered, eh? You know damn well that any loose slates are to be fixed straight away, especially on this side, above the conservatory. Same thing happened last winter, didn't it—except that nobody was unlucky enough to be standing here at that time.'

'I didn't know anything was loose,' said the young man reasonably.

Warbeck's yellow eyes glinted. 'From now on you'll know every creaking joist, every patch of damp, every crack and weakness in this house, and you'll put it right before ever I hear of it, or you and your subnormal twin can pack your bags. Understand?'

'He's not my twin,' answered Gil coldly.

Martin's mouth thinned into lines of contempt. 'I see little difference between you.'

Gil made no answer but turned and stalked off to the toolshed, pushing past a flustered Dorcas on his way through the kitchen.

'What's happened?' she hissed.

'He's a prize bastard,' muttered the handyman.

'Been getting at you, has he?' Dorcas

tsked to herself. 'He's always been a miserable sod,' she said soothingly. 'It's not your fault, after all. Slates do come off in windy weather ...' She paused suddenly and frowned. 'Funny thing though, there's no wind today.'

'For God's sake, Ma, go on. He's waiting,' urged Pandy.

'Let the bugger wait. Let him bleed.' declared Dorcas defiantly. 'Bothering me just when I'm doing his potroast.'

Nevertheless within fifteen minutes she had Martin bandaged up and had sent for the doctor. It was not until after the doctor had left that Gil knocked at the study door with a piece of disturbing information.

'There's no slates off,' he stated simply. 'Not one.'

'Don't be so damned stupid. What's that if not a slate?' Martin pointed irritably to the fragments lying on his desk. 'Don't try to absolve yourself ...'

'Certainly it's a slate,' agreed Gil calmly, 'but it's not one of ours. They're all in place. Not a gap anywhere. This one's not even the same colour.'

Martin's forehead creased into a frown with the realisation that this was true. The slate was a sort of reddish brown, while Forest Rift was roofed with grey.

Gil watched his employer's face, pleased to prove him wrong. He knew better than to expect an apology but it felt good to see Martin confused.

'Wonder where it came from?' The question hung ominously in the air for a moment. 'Slates don't just materialise, do they?' persisted Gil.

Martin cast an uneasy look at his handyman. Where indeed?

'You've got work to do, get on with it. I might still fire you, if only for insolence.'

'I only said that slates don't appear out of nowhere.'

'I can work that out for myself,' snapped Warbeck. 'Now get out.'

He sat down and poured himself a stiff drink. An alarming thought had crossed his mind. Helen's bedroom window was one of those above the conservatory. She could have seen him standing beneath and, although her room was somewhat to the right, perhaps with a flick of the wrist she could have angled the slate to hit him. Was it possible? Could she do such a thing? But no. No, he was being foolish. Where would Helen get hold of a slate? She had not left her bedroom in two days—had she?

Martin snorted. He would get to the bottom of it, sooner or later. If Helen wanted to play rough he would be pleased to oblige. She couldn't remain up there forever. She would have to come out sometime and when she did there would be hell to pay.

He got up and winced a little. The gash was really beginning to smart. Damn her. Thank God he would soon be free of her and comfortably settled with Cordelia.

Cordey read the letter through a second time, feeling a blend of pleasure and astonishment. How very eloquent and how terribly flattering. Such a shy young man too. George Coleman might be a dynamo in the courtroom but in Cordelia's presence he reverted to a tongue-tied, awkward youth—which must have been painful for a newly qualified barrister. Self-control, quick wits and cool thinking were the tools of his trade, yet they deserted him the moment he encountered Cordey, leaving him almost unable to form a coherent sentence—the side-effects, she supposed, of overwhelming love.

However George displayed far more daring on paper. He was lavish with his compliments and sincere to a frightening degree. There was no trace of banter, nothing prosaic or casual in this letter—it was all tumultuous stuff. And it was the third one in four days! Cordelia could not help being pleased. George's soul-baring made Martin seem rather mundane. The letter aroused in Cordelia an old romanticism which time and Henry Willard had smothered but which was not quite dead.

She folded it up and tucked it in her purse, still marvelling that appearances could be so deceptive. George had always struck her as a tame and colourless person and he had never merited much of her attention. Of course he would have to be told, gently but firmly, that there was no hope for him, although she felt reluctant to discard him outright.

Cordey toyed with the idea of allowing him to visit her just once, decided that to encourage him would be cruel and then changed her mind once more as vanity got the better of her. He was quite attractive in a gentle sort of way—nothing flashy but pleasant to look at—and she was seized with a heartless urge to keep him dangling for a while. It's so nice to feel wanted.

She smiled at her reflection in the mirror and patted the smooth coils of her hair. Oh, the joy of being pursued, the power, the gratification. She rang for her maid and ordered tea with angel-cake and gingerbread. The tempo of her life was rising daily from the dreary, plodding years with Henry to a sudden, swirling waltz. She had so much money—and already her home was looking brighter and richer because of it. And she had admirers—first Martin and now George. Before her was the prospect of a new house in London. It was like being a girl again. The future twinkled with promise and Cordey was resolved not to make a second mistake. There would be no more mediocrity, no more wasted life.

Cordey toyed with the cameo brooch nestling in the lace at her throat and frowned slightly. It would be unwise to tell Martin about George and his letters. His jealousy was liable to make a great issue out of a little harmless dalliance. She sighed and poured herself some tea, relaxing into the deep green velvet of her new settee. How quickly life had changed and she had done it all with suet pudding.

'Treacherous beast!' Helen scowled at the carpet as she sat morosely on the edge of her four-poster bed, wearing slippers and an old pink dressing-gown. 'I'm not sure which of them I hate most.'

Laurel listened and said nothing.

'How could he go off like that? How dare he make a fool out of me!'

'I don't think he intended that,' interrupted Mrs Jay.

'Of course he did. They're all the same, damn them.'

'But don't you think Martin has been making a fool of you all these years? All the different women he's had—how is it that you could put up with that?'

'That's different. I don't give a damn about him or what he does. I don't want him. It's convenient that he gets what he needs elsewhere.'

'But you do want Michael?'

'Not any more,' snorted Helen. 'How can you have any regard for a man who slinks off and leaves you at the first sign of trouble? And of course Martin is just revelling in this. He enjoys seeing me humiliated.'

'I think he's too busy licking his own wounds.'

Helen got up and paced fretfully back and forth between the window and the bed. Her tired face, around which the blond hair hung lank and messy, was enlivened only by the bright anger in her eyes. Michael had made all kinds of promises and now he had disappeared. Helen was not accustomed to being deserted. She had always enjoyed a measure of power where men were concerned. Even Martin was subject to her whim—if only because of her money. To be thus helplessly abandoned by the first man she had ever really wanted was infuriating.

'I don't think he's gone because he's tired of you,' soothed Laurel.

Helen stared balefully at her. 'Why then?'

'Maybe he's afraid of Martin.'

'Cowardly too,' snorted Helen.

'Your husband has a fearful temper.'

Helen flopped down on the bed again. 'Hot air,' she said tersely, 'and I can prove it.'

The dark girl's eyes widened. 'How?'

'Pass me my notepaper and pen.'

Silently Laurel handed her the stationery.

'Let's see how much fear he can strike into my brother.'

A slow grin lit Mrs Jay's face.

Helen stared thoughtfully into space for a few moments and then began swiftly to write. She blotted the ink, then took another critical look at the note.

'Yes,' she said at length, sealing it into its envelope, 'I think that's quite effective. Will you deliver it for me?'

'Of course.' The girl took the note and slipped it into her handbag. Then she said, 'I know you're upset, Helen, but I wish you would eat something.'

'I'm not upset, I'm angry.'

'There's not much difference.'

'And I've got no appetite.'

'You'll make yourself ill. I don't want to see you waste away over this.'

'I've no intention of wasting away,' retorted Helen defiantly. 'That would be a real victory for them, wouldn't it?'

'Exactly.' Laurel seemed relieved.

'I just wish there was something I could do,' continued Helen.

'Sleep on it. Something may occur to you.' Laurel got up and went to the door. 'I'm going into Meadstock this afternoon. Can I fetch you anything?'

'No, but don't forget the letter.'

'Oh don't worry, I won't.'

Helen smiled for the first time in days.

'I'm very lucky to have a friend like you.'

Laurel turned away and didn't seem to hear as she slipped out of the room and disappeared down the stairs. Behind her Helen slid the bolt firmly home—to keep her husband out.

SIXTEEN

September 22nd. 1903

Dearest Peter,

I am distraught. I'm sure you know that my husband has discovered my friendship with Mr Conran—a perfectly innocent friendship, I might add. In his rage, Martin struck me repeatedly and I have been locked in my bedroom for nearly four days. I am too terrified to come out for fear of further violence, and I cannot eat for the state of my nerves.

What is worse, Mr Conran appears to have vanished, which is horribly distressing, as I had counted on his support. It is a frightful betrayal and I do so hope that I can rely on you and dear Katie to come immediately and reason with my husband and offer me some comfort. Please do not inform

Papa, for I've no wish to alarm him.
Your loving sister,
Helen.

Peter frowned at the note and then handed it to Katie, who read it suspiciously.

'Well,' she said at length, 'Helen might have expected him to be angry.'

'No one,' replied Peter dourly, 'has any right to ill-treat a member of my family.'

Katie cocked an eyebrow. 'I sense a touch of exaggeration in this note,' she said wisely. 'A bit theatrical, don't you think? overly piteous?'

Peter didn't think so. Like many otherwise intelligent men, he believed implicitly in the honesty of women and was grieved to hear such cynicism from his wife. Partly underlying this faith was the conviction that Helen (who, he thought, had been stupid all her life) was incapable of guile.

'I'm going out there.'

'Now?'

'Right now.'

Katie watched him storm out to the

stables. Peter to the rescue. She was not inclined to argue—it was never any use when he had the bit between his teeth. She picked up a cloth and began polishing the sherry barrels, feeling a faint stirring of sympathy for Martin and hoping that he would not be at home when Peter arrived.

George Coleman perched nervously on the edge of the sofa, clutching his bunch of flowers. His finest suit was immaculately pressed, his shoes lovingly polished and his hair parted with precision. None of these preparations however made him feel any less awkward. It had taken George fully two hours to wash and dress for this very important occasion and he had reached that uncomfortable pinnacle of smartness which renders one almost afraid to breathe in case the whole ensemble collapses. He moved only gingerly lest he wrinkle his suit, repeatedly adjusted his tie and ran a nervous hand over his chin to check that no lightning growth of stubble had appeared. It was not normally George's habit to be so fussy about his appearance but today was special. It was all for Cordey. It was terribly important that everything should be perfect if he was to make an impression on her.

She was taking a very long time. The maid had said that Mrs Willard was doing her hair and George ventured to assume that she wished to look nice for him.

'Mr Coleman, you do look smart!'

George's head jerked up. He blinked in confusion and leapt to his feet.

'Uh, Mrs Willard, I, uh, Cordelia ...'

Cordey smiled and pointed to the flowers. 'Are those for me?'

Coleman thrust the roses at her. 'Just a few, um, a little, you know ...'

'How lovely!' She sniffed them and sighed. 'You're too kind.'

He looked pleased but didn't manage to say anything.

'Well, uh,' Cordey hesitated, 'I think we'd better put these in water to keep them fresh. How did you know I like yellow roses?'

'Oh, um, I can't remember. Someone

must have told me.' He gazed at her helplessly, groping for something interesting to say.

'I think we should have tea first of all, don't you? Do sit down and make yourself at home.'

He seated himself stiffly on the sofa once more as she rang for the maid. It was just not possible to relax. He couldn't permit himself to sit back and cross his legs, not in her imposing presence. The maid appeared and Cordey handed her the roses.

'Put them in water, carefully now, and bring us afternoon tea, dear, will you? A nice selection, please. I'm sure Mr Coleman's got a fine appetite.'

'Oh, don't go to any trouble, not for my sake ...' stammered George.

'Nonsense. I know how to look after a strong, healthy man,' beamed Cordelia. 'Now then, you must tell me all about your work. I have the greatest admiration for anyone who can cope with the intricacies of the law.'

George was profoundly grateful to her for this. His work was one subject on which he could talk with ease. She settled herself in an armchair facing him and listened, apparently riveted, while he outlined some of the basic structures of English law. He was deep in murder and manslaughter when the tea arrived and Cordey managed to distract him with a chunk of walnut cake.

'Of course, I'm being terribly brief. I haven't even begun to explain the basics ...'

'Barely scratched the surface,' agreed Cordelia hastily.

'I mean, one has to study for years and years to obtain mastery of such a vast subject.'

'Naturally. You must find it exhausting.'

'No, no. It's very stimulating.'

'Really,' murmured Cordey. 'Gingerbread?'

George accepted a piece. He was finally beginning to relax.

'Do you have anything to do with divorce?' she asked suddenly.

He paused in mid-munch. 'Divorce? Well, no. I can't say I've had any experience of that. Sad business, of course.'

'Tragic,' nodded Cordelia. 'How easy is it to get one?'

Coleman's brown eyes regarded her with puzzlement over the rim of his cup. He swallowed a mouthful of tea and cleared his throat.

'Well, if there are strong grounds, easily proven, it's not too difficult. Why do you ask?'

'Morbid curiosity, I suppose. Of course Henry and I were so happy together. I can't imagine anything more awful than the breakup of a marriage. Upsetting, don't you think?'

'Yes, but you mustn't concern yourself with other people's troubles,' soothed George, charmed at her sensitivity.

'And I always believed lawyers were shrewd,' she thought to herself. 'Ah, well, love makes fools of us all.'

'I expect you miss him a great deal,' ventured George. 'I mean, you must get lonely.'

'Oh yes,' she agreed. 'Loneliness is the

first and greatest problem. I am fortunate that Henry left me comfortably provided for, but one does need company. I do enjoy having someone intelligent to talk to.'

A moment's silence fell and there hovered between them the unmentioned subject of George's letters. He felt vaguely silly about them now. It was, to say the least, peculiar to sit there exchanging platonic small-talk after the writing of so much passion.

He began to stammer again. 'I, uh, you don't ...? I mean, I hope you weren't offended at what I wrote. It was a bit forward of me, I suppose—with you so recently bereaved.'

Cordelia considered her reply carefully. She fancied she would quite like to keep him as a sort of part-time admirer but it was important to avoid getting seriously involved. Martin wouldn't like that.

'Forward? Well, perhaps, but in the most charming manner. I was quite overwhelmed. No one has ever written to me in that way before.'

George's blush deepened.

'And I won't pretend that I wasn't pleased,' continued Cordey, 'but you must understand that I am still in mourning for my husband. It would be both callous and selfish of me to allow myself any more involvements—for the time being.'

George computed that as a gesture of discreet encouragement. Naturally he would have to wait awhile but he could tolerate that. Things were going far better than he expected. She was really quite easy to talk to. Perhaps he was in with a chance.

'I've always admired you,' he blurted suddenly.

She smiled benignly. 'What a dear you are. You realise, I suppose, that there is a considerable difference in our ages?'

'I think you're more woman than any simpering twenty-year-old,' declared George boldly.

'My, my,' purred Cordey, offering him a plate of Bath buns, 'I do believe you're quite a handful beneath that bashful exterior.'

George's chest swelled and he chomped nonchalantly on his Bath bun. 'Would you mind if I called on you again sometime?'

'That would be lovely but I think we should arrange it in advance, don't you? No, uh, surprise visits. For propriety's sake, you understand.'

George nodded earnestly. 'Quite right. We don't want to start any rumours.'

'Indeed we don't,' she thought. Martin would not be pleased if this ever got back to him.

Coleman left about an hour later, far bouncier than when he came in. He felt suddenly primeval, rampant and filled with hope.

From her parlour window Cordelia watched him stride manfully off down the street and smiled to herself. It was quite fun to have a young man in tow, some extra entertainment to sustain her until the move to London.

A few flakes of mud-coloured paint still clung loosely to the old outhouse door. It was a crude, slatted door, infested with woodworm, and to the right of it was set a small window, filmy with the grime of years. The walls were concealed by a thick growth of ivy and convolvulus, so that the old shed, which might otherwise have been an eyesore, appeared almost quaint. It stood beside the wash-house at the back of the stables and hardly anyone had been inside since the day Gordon first looked the house over and decided to buy it.

She pushed tentatively at the old door. It was evidently not locked but the hinges had rusted up, making it stiff to open. She leant her full weight against the rough wood and there was a shuddering sound as it edged inwards. Another hard shove and there was a gap wide enough to squeeze through.

Inside, a shaft of sunlight from the window sliced through the gloom, il-luminating the swirls of dust stirred up by her feet. As her eyes became accustomed to the murky light she saw that the ivy had squirmed its way through cracks in the walls and roof and was gradually coiling dark tendrils down to the floor. There were garden rakes and hoes, an old ploughshare and some metal buckets stacked in one corner, and to her left a great iron-bound cartwheel was suspended from two hooks driven into the wall. Beside it hung some lengths of heavy chain and a great harness that looked as if it might once have been worn by a shire-horse. The place smelt of age without decay, fusty and forgotten—as indeed it was—with a staleness that was somehow peaceful. It must at one time have been much used by some predecessor of Gil and Jacob.

None of this was of any use to her. She frowned, her gaze flitting about, hoping for some lucky find. It was not until her glance dropped to the floor that she noticed the object lying all but buried in the thick dust beneath the window.

Bending down, she lifted it, blowing away the dirt to get a better look. The thing was heavy, cold, and a slow smile lifted the corners of her mouth as she realised what it was. It must have lain there, unused, for decades—the very thing she needed. This precious find, this horrible anachronism, was tailor-made for her purpose. Carefully she set it down in the dust again and covered it with a pile of sacking.

Suddenly she remembered the time. They would be returning soon—Martin from his ride and the stablehands from Meadstock, where they went for supplies every Saturday morning. Quickly she slid out through the door and tugged it shut behind her, then hurried into the house, brushing the dust and cobwebs from her hair and clothes.

SEVENTEEN

The forest turned rusty-amber, a billowing cloud of fire colours. Early October was bright and windy and Gil had already started sawing up logs for the winter, while Laurel rushed off early each morning, armed with paints and canvas, to capture this last burst of brilliance before dreary November set in.

Any thoughts Martin might have had about tackling Helen over the slate incident were dispelled by Peter's visit. There was a short scuffle, in which Martin came off worst and thought it wisest to back down before he suffered real damage. When Helen had finally emerged from her room later that evening she found her husband nursing a black eye. Thereafter they ignored each other completely. He had not yet told Helen of his plan to divorce her. He was saving that for just the right moment, when it would have most impact. He stored it away like a special treat to enjoy later and although it was less than three weeks since he had learned of Helen's affair this split in his marriage didn't seem at all new. It had always been there, ticking away just below the surface, waiting for a flashpoint.

He had almost forgotten the episode in the conservatory when a second outrage occurred.

It was late—about 2 a.m. He had stayed up to finish a specially fine bottle of ruby port and sent Pandy off to bed without checking that she had done everything she was supposed to. And look what he got for it. Damned girl, idle little slut. He fumed, tripping on the stairs. She hadn't bothered to light the gas on the landing, or in his bedroom. The whole house was dark and he had already slipped twice, bruising his shins as he fell. He swore and stumbled back down to the kitchen in search of the matches. There were only three left and he used two of them to light his way upstairs. Reaching his room, he kicked the door shut behind him and began groping awkwardly round the walls, looking for the gas brackets.

Martin wasn't used to this room, he had only moved into it two days before. It was once Celia's and had not been used since she left. He had taken it over in order to be as far from Helen as possible—which was fine, except that now he couldn't remember where to find the lights. He stumbled, cursing, over some piece of furniture and threw out his arms to save himself from falling. This was ridiculous. His temper mounted. By God, Pandy would cop it in the morning.

The gas-taps must be on the other side. He started to move carefully across the centre of the room and—tripped over something. Something which bit him! Slashed him! Something ripped at the flesh of his left leg. A cold, serrated something—like a huge saw.

Martin didn't quite scream. It halted in his throat and turned to a gasp, more of fear than pain. There was a warm, slow trickle of what must be blood oozing down his leg from some stinging injury about three inches above the ankle. He could feel the blood creeping down and soaking into his sock.

Seconds ticked by, drew out, graduated to minutes and, when nothing more happened, nothing moved, he began to fumble for the last match. With shaking fingers, he struck it.

The feeble light lasted only a few seconds. Only long enough to distinguish the outline of the thing on the floor. The black, square, iron thing, with its spring and its teeth and its chain, carefully spread open by some purposeful hand for the snaring of the unsuspecting. A mantrap.

Martin Warbeck heard himself whimper. A lost and fearful sound, as if a full-blown scream would be too risky and bring down unknown horrors on his back—something or someone just out of sight, someone who stood grinning in the shadows with malicious eyes fixed on the back of his neck.

In the same light, just before it drew too near his fingers to hold, he saw the gas brackets. Two of them, to his right, above the bed. He edged round the black object, felt for the tap, turned it and put the dying match to the gas.

No mistake. There it lay, primed and ready to spring. Old and splotched with rust. A thing not used in this district since his father's youth. A wicked, evil thing, designed for the poacher or trespasser. The squire's watchdog. The mantrap.

He sat on his bed and stared at it. Perhaps he had a guardian angel, for narrowly, with the purest of luck, he had missed the clamping of the iron teeth, missed the step that would set his foot on the crossbar and spring. A shudder rose from his gut and spread all over his body. He had caught his leg on those teeth but from the outside. Escaped, but only just.

Who? Fright was wavering, growing into anger. She must be raving bloody mad. She should be certified, locked away, the vicious bitch. It was just like her to think of something so medieval, so crude. It was positively ghoulish. Helen's face hovered before him, changing from one guise to the next. The flirt, the idiot, the petulant, whining and deceitful wife. The malicious, cunning bitch.

He took from the wardrobe a walking cane, drove it onto the spring-plate of the trap and—nothing happened. He peered closely at it. The spring mechanism was rusted through, broken. How typically incompetent of her. However the fact that the trap didn't work was beside the point—the intention was there just the same.

Martin's face looked drawn, haggard in the gaslight. How could she? There was no question of accident here, unlike the business in the conservatory. Nothing could be more deliberate or more wicked. She had set this thing and extinguished all the lights in the hope that he would blunder into it. Everything seemed quite simple to Martin. After all, Helen had never been subtle.

He took the trap downstairs and threw it outside the back door, unable to bear the thought of having it in the room all night. He fetched some warm water and dabbed gingerly at the gash with a towel, cleaned it as best he could and bandaged it up. Then he lay down on his bed without bothering to undress.

The witch. If she was capable of this what else might she do? Even with the windows and doors locked he couldn't rest easy. Of course it just wasn't possible to stay in the same house with her any longer. In the morning he would have the pleasure of telling her that she was about to be divorced. Telling her that he didn't need her money or her, because he had a better woman to go to. Telling her that she could have the house, and Rosalie, and her boring circle of vapid friends, because he was going to London with Cordelia—and the whole Strickland clan could go to hell.

'Where did you get that?'

Jacob blinked vacantly at his brother and grinned, holding up the trap for him to see.

'I know,' persisted Gil, 'but where?

Where did you find it?'

Jacob waved an arm vaguely in the direction of the house. Gil shook his head. 'Picked it up in the woods, I suppose. Give it here.'

Reluctantly his brother handed over the trap.

'Doesn't work anyway,' grunted Gil. 'Anybody can see that. Just as well too. Father got caught in one of these when he was young. That's why he walked with a limp. Do you remember him—how he used to take us fishing?'

Jacob grinned again.

'No, well, doesn't matter any more. If you don't remember then you don't miss him.'

Jacob pointed to the trap, hoping he could keep it.

'No, you don't want this. These things are dangerous, see. Bad for you. We'll get rid of it when we go out this morning. Like to pick some mushrooms?'

His brother nodded eagerly, then, suddenly subdued, he mumbled, 'No spotted ones.'

'Right! Nearly poisoned yourself last week, didn't you?'

Jacob looked contrite.

'Come on, get your jacket and we'll go.'

They took the woodland footpath which began just behind the stables and were more than a mile away by the time Martin got up. He headed straight for the back door and stamped outside in search of the trap. He was furious to find it gone and assumed instantly that Helen had hidden it, like a felon removing the evidence.

He found her in the dining-room, finishing her breakfast with an air of innocence which brought a curl to his lip. He walked silently to the table and sat down. Helen glanced up without any sign of surprise, then went on eating. Martin helped himself to a portion of haddock, all the time surveying his wife, weighing up her mood. She didn't seem even aware that he was watching her, let alone disappointed at the failure of her little ambush. Very good, Helen, very cool. Quite out of character of course, but good nonetheless.

Suddenly he pushed his chair back and swung his leg up, landing a booted foot heavily on the table. His teacup overturned and Helen jumped.

'Well?' he demanded.

She stared at him, lost for something to say.

Martin tugged up his trouser leg to reveal the scruffy bandage he had applied the night before. 'Disappointed? Just a little cut, I'm afraid. Sorry I couldn't oblige you with something more permanent.'

Helen slowly put down her knife and fork, eyes fixed warily on her husband. 'What are you ...?'

'Oh, yes. Innocence incarnate,' hissed Martin.

'I don't understand.'

'... don't understand,' he mimicked viciously.

'Martin, stop this. Whatever you've done to your leg, it's nothing to do with me.'

'It didn't work, you brainless bitch,' he roared, ignoring Pandy who sidled in to collect some dirty dishes off the sideboard and lingered as long as she could over it.

'How dare you! And take your damned foot off my table,' snapped his wife.

'It was rusty,' continued Martin, 'broken ...'

'What was?' cut in Helen sharply. 'For God's sake be rational.

Martin removed his foot from the table and leaned back in his chair, glowering at her. 'A mantrap,' he growled, 'of all things. I didn't think you had that much imagination.'

Her face took on an appalled expression. 'You're mad,' she observed quietly. 'You really are.'

'What have you done with it, eh? Where's it gone? Prudent of you to get rid of the evidence.'

Helen moved to get up. 'I'm not staying ...'

'Sit down,' bellowed Martin. Helen sat and Pandy dropped a handful of cutlery. 'And what are you hovering round for? All ears and mouth, just like your mother,' he snarled and the girl fled without stopping to pick anything up.

'First you tried to kill me in the

conservatory, then you had your brother assault me for no good reason and now this. Beneath all the bows and frills you're really quite a little savage.'

'When my father hears about this you're going to be the most sorry man ...' she began.

This seemed to him like a good moment to break his precious piece of news to her. He was just in the mood to enjoy it to the full.

'Your father and his pathetic opinions no longer affect me.'

She looked at him blankly.

'Because I'm going to divorce you,' announced Martin sweetly. 'I've already made arrangements to marry Cordelia Willard.'

Helen's reaction left him utterly deflated. She considered his words calmly for some moments, then, 'I think that's the best thing you can do. Rosalie and I will go over to Papa's for a few months while things get settled.'

Martin's face fell. 'Aren't you even ...?'

'Upset? No. I'm really past caring and

the thought of being rid of you seems very attractive.'

'I'll get you for infidelity,' said Martin hotly. 'You'll have such a reputation in this district ...'

'I believe I have one already.' Helen placidly folded her napkin and got to her feet. On her way out she turned at the door and surveyed him scornfully. 'If my reputation is weighed against yours I know who will emerge looking dirtiest. I've had one short-lived affair, Martin. I don't suppose you can remember all of yours.'

'It's different for a woman. You'll find out,' he shouted after her.

Helen didn't much care—about him or Conran or her 'friends' and what they would say. The change in her personality over the past few weeks was evidenced most strongly by a growing conviction that nobody was stainless and everybody was treacherous. She bustled up the stairs and rang for Pandy to get Rosalie ready and help them pack. Gerald at least would be pleased to have their company.

Chloe Levermore didn't know whether to be pleased or furious that Martin had slapped her daughter. In one way it justified her opinion of him and ensured that Virginia would have nothing more to do with her common in-laws. On the other hand it was insulting—a gesture of contempt against Virginia and therefore, thought Chloe, against the Levermore family.

She spread the details with an awesome and single-minded malice, designed to make Martin look as black as possible. Amusement turned to shock in Meadstock as Pandy's tattlings, usually dismissed as servants' gossip, were suddenly backed with more authority.

'I'm assured by a reliable source,' said Chloe in the bread shop one morning, 'that he ill-treats his wife shamefully. So much so that her brother has been forced to intervene on at least one occasion, and as you know, Mr Strickland—a great friend of mine—is by nature a very mild man. I can't imagine what that creature must have done to poor Mrs Warbeck to make Peter so angry. And,' she paused for effect as her audience fairly drooled curiosity, 'he makes wild accusations. He has actually suggested that the poor woman is trying to kill him.'

The other three ladies gasped in unison.

'Yes,' continued Chloe, 'and in the most bizarre manner. Apparently he came down to breakfast one morning and began raving about some kind of trap. Of course dear Helen had no idea what it was all about and, fearing that his sanity might be in doubt, she packed up and left him that very day. She's taken the child and gone back to her father, which I feel is very wise, don't you?'

'Oh very wise,' chorused the ladies earnestly.

'There's more,' went on Chloe, loving their pop-eyed attention. 'You may recall that Helen had a friend staying with her? An artist? Well, she's gone. Disappeared. I think it's very worrying under the circumstances, don't you?'

'Ominous,' agreed Mr Platt from behind the counter. 'Do you mind having a milk loaf today? We've run out of wholemeal.'

'Anything,' said Chloe impatiently, anxious to get on with her tale. 'I mean to say, Mr Warbeck claims she's gone to Stennack now that Helen has left Forest Rift, but I really don't know whether to believe it. Lord forbid that anything's happened to the poor dear.'

The ladies tsked to each other and looked concerned.

'What will happen to that house now?' asked one of them. 'I mean, it's not his any more, is it?'

'Well no, and of course he says he's going to divorce poor Helen. I rather think it should be the other way around, don't you? Obviously Gerald Strickland won't let him stay there now. Someone told me he's been given fourteen days to make other arrangements. And of course you and I all know what those will be,' ended Chloe confidentially.

The ladies nodded. 'Oh, her,' said one of them contemptuously. 'That's well enough for her. She has the most appalling taste in men. I mean, fancy marrying Henry Willard for a start.'

Martin's unpopularity was growing by the hour and Cordelia, aware that the condition can be contagious and unprepared to become a social outcast, had already begun to wonder if it might not be wise to cast a predatory eye elsewhere. Additionally, might it not be true that he ill-treated his wife? The last thing Cordey wanted was a violent husband and Martin was beginning to sound a bit irrational—dangerous in fact. And then one morning, in the post, came the alternative she needed. A proposal from George.

Martin knew nothing of this until he called at Cordelia's house some days later, only to be told that Mrs Coleman, latterly the widowed Mrs Willard, was in Venice on honeymoon and would not be back for six months. It took him fully two days to digest this incredible treachery and then the panic set in.

As the full horror of his situation became clear Martin's first thought was to attempt a reconciliation with his wife, but she was never 'at home'. His notes were ignored and when his persistence became too wearisome Helen sent Peter round to Forest Rift again, to inform her husband that he was welcome to proceed with the divorce because she had no intention of ever returning to him.

The fourteen days ticked inexorably away and he didn't know where to turn. He had just £7 in the bank and bills which amounted to £123 11s 4d. Everyone, it seemed, had turned his back on him, including his brother.

EIGHTEEN

Eight days. Just eight days and he would be homeless, penniless. No one would lend him anything. No one offered him a job. A shadow loomed drearily in his mind. It was called the workhouse.

He ran a hand distractedly over the stubble on his face. Three days' growth. Why shave? Why wash? Despair comes easily to people who have no resources of their own. This was the sting in the tail of dependence—this helplessness when the props were removed.

The bottle was still half-full. That was something. Just as long as there was another swig things weren't altogether unbearable. His gaze swivelled groggily round the room. He had barely ceased drinking for forty-eight hours and bouts of wakeful misery alternated with periods of broken sleep. It was cold, he realised suddenly, even in bed—or the twisted, knotted chaos of his bed. Martin couldn't quite muster the co-ordination to sort out the tangle of sheets and blankets caused by his own restless thrashing. There was no fire. Pandy hadn't lit the fire, hadn't brought him breakfast or lunch. He blinked, stupidly, trying to remember when last he ate. The skin felt taut and stretched across his cheeks, head heavy, mouth slack. What he needed was something to soak it up. Something crunchy, savoury. Dry toast.

He lurched out of bed, grasping the headboard for support, and tottered across to the bell-pull, yanking it hard. Minutes passed and no one came. He rang again, sharp, impatient jerks. Nothing.

'Blast you,' he yelled, glaring up at the spot where the bell cord disappeared through the wall en route to the kitchen. 'Are you damn' well deaf?' His voice rose and cracked, hoarse with booze and temper. He fumbled with the door, cursing that it wouldn't open, then realised that he had bolted himself in. He slammed back the bolts, flung open the heavy oak door and reeled out onto the landing, snarling for Pandy.

There was dead silence. He thumped against the banister, glaring down into the hall below, a swaying, scruffy figure in a sweat-soaked shirt and rumpled trousers. Martin Warbeck, who had always been so particular about his looks.

'Where the hell are you?' he slurred. 'Eh? I'm still ...' he leaned precariously over the rail, 'still in charge here. Still give the orders. I'm not gone yet. Bet you can't bloody wait, can you? Just dying for me to go.' There was still no answer. 'Cowering in the kitchen, are you? Stupid bitch. Pandy!!' The roar echoed round empty rooms and passages. 'I, I still pay your wages ...' His voice dropped, uncertain. 'I do, you're lucky to work for me ...'

'But that's the point, isn't it?' a voice interrupted calmly. 'You don't.'

'Eh?' Warbeck squinted down at the figure who strolled out into the hallway. 'Don't? What?'

'Don't pay their wages.' Gil smiled

pleasantly. 'No one's been paid anything for a fortnight.'

Martin peered down at him and said nothing.

'Not that I mind,' continued the handyman, 'and Jacob, well, he doesn't understand money. Doesn't know what it's for.' He paused and shook his head in feigned sorrow. 'But Pandy and Dorcas, they minded. They wanted paying.' He beamed up at Martin. 'You know how mercenary women can be.'

'They're not ...'

'Gone. Yes,' replied the young man patiently. 'That's what I'm trying to tell you. They went yesterday morning, early.'

Warbeck sank down to the floor, his back to the banisters, and drew his knees up almost to his chin. Gone. No one to cook for him. His eyes fixed sorrowfully on a picture of his mother, which hung on the opposite wall. She was, he thought, the only decent woman he ever knew. Gil's news had sobered him up somewhat and he regarded Hannah's picture with misery turning to anger. Women. They were all cast in the same mould. Helen, Cordelia, Rachel, Laurel. They would leave you, rob you, double-cross you, even murder you. Right now he'd like to kill the lot of them, just like Rachel Shea.

Martin sprawled there, brooding, for fifteen or twenty minutes before hauling himself upright to plod downstairs in search of food. At least he still had the stablehands to chop wood and tend the horses. He could manage for a few days. His mind refused even to consider what might happen when the few days were up.

It took Katie a good deal of coaxing and argument to persuade Peter to offer his brother-in-law a job. The tussle went on for days as Strickland dug his heels in, determined to let Martin go down the drain where, said Peter, he belonged. It was unlike her husband to be either stubborn or ungenerous and Katie felt certain that her persistence would eventually pay off. She was right. Strickland finally relented and agreed to offer Martin a job as cellarman, in return for his bed and board at the Maple. It was Peter's fond hope that Martin would refuse the offer but, as Katie said, he just couldn't afford to do that.

The house had never known so much silence. All through the years there had been the sounds of human activity, human life. Clatter from the scullery and chatter from the parlour, rustling skirts and a maid's high-pitched giggle, men's voices discussing business, horses and sometimes women. Only in the dead of night had there been silence such as this and even then, sometimes, there were whispers in the dark and the creaking of springs.

He stood in the study, remembering, and absently stroking the polished walnut top of Gordon's desk. His fingers left tracks in the dust, for no one tended these matters now that the maids were gone.

Forest Rift wasn't his any more. No longer his home. Well, to be truthful, he had lost it long ago but it always felt like his house, even after Gerald bought it. Martin had never before been sentimental. He had always regarded people and things in strictly practical terms—of greater or lesser advantage to his own well-being. Today, for the first time, he really experienced the wrench of separation from the familiar.

His clothes were packed haphazardly into the small trunks which waited in the hall. The process of packing, of locking the trunks, had upset him a great deal, for it had such an air of finality. The good life, it seemed, was well and truly over.

Martin turned reluctantly and dawdled out into the hall. Peter was waiting outside with the pony and trap, sensitive enough to perceive Warbeck's feelings and patient enough not to hurry him. Martin picked up the trunks by their leather straps, stepped outside and, with the merest hesitation, jerked the door shut behind him. Strickland reached down for one of the trunks, his manner laudably matter-of-fact in view of the discomfort he felt. With all Martin's worldly goods safely stowed on the back seat Peter made haste to get back to town as quickly as possible.

The journey into Meadstock was tedious.

Strickland's attempts at conversation were strained and Martin was unresponsive. He had voiced stiff thanks for the offer of work, edged with resentment and stung pride. The situation humiliated Warbeck and embarrassed his new employer, worsened by the fact that each knew how the other felt about it.

Martin was also furious with his brother. His own flesh and blood had made no offer of help. It almost frightened him to realise that mediocre, boring old Neil could be so unyielding. A touch of the old man there, thought Martin bitterly. Once you crossed him he never really forgave you.

Peter didn't ask him if the room was all right. He was not offering any choices and Martin knew better than to grumble. Not for the present at least. This might only be a temporary situation in any case. Perhaps, when the storm had died down, things would improve. He had of course withdrawn his plans to divorce Helen, so she was making arrangements to divorce him. Martin hoped that she wouldn't go through with it. Maybe she would miss him—especially when it became apparent that there were not, after all, so many second husbands in stock, anxious to replace him.

Nevertheless he surveyed the room, its plain furnishings and dormer-windows, with distaste. It was clean and fairly comfortable but the first word that sprang to Martin's mind was 'shabby'. Katie had lit the fire and placed a bowl of fruit on the bedside table as a welcoming gesture. There were several scatter rugs on the floor and a china jug and washbasin on the dressing table. Hardly luxury, he thought sourly as he began to unpack and arrange his belongings.

Lunchtime came and went with no suggestion of food. He was amazed to find that the Stricklands ate their main meal at four in the afternoon, between lunchtime and evening opening hours, and by the time they sat down to a steaming Lancashire hotpot Martin was too ravenous to remember that he disliked this particular dish.

'We don't even attempt to eat at

lunchtime or mid-evening,' Katie said. 'We'd be in and out serving rounds between each bite.'

'Plays hell with your digestion,' Peter added.

'You mean it's always like this?' Martin was alarmed. 'Don't tell me everybody in this trade does the same?'

Katie shrugged and poured him a glass of ale. 'I don't know how other people manage. Some of them have more staff and so they can take breaks in rotation. We have to eat when we can.'

'Been doing it this way for years. You'll get accustomed to it,' Peter grinned, 'eventually.'

Martin tried to hide his dismay. Mealtimes at Forest Rift had been something sacred, to be approached with due ceremony, savoured, lingered over. Dinner was a minor social event, not a refuelling operation between one rush and the next. It was going to be hard for a man who had led a pampered, leisured life to adjust to the frenzied pace and odd hours of a busy licensed house.

'I'll take you downstairs around five o'clock and show you what to do. By the way, we don't expect you to serve in the bar,' Peter said cautiously. 'Not yet anyway. It'll be all cellarwork to begin with.'

'We didn't think you'd like serving ...' began Katie.

'No. I wouldn't.'

'But if you did change your mind anytime I think you'd find the social atmosphere quite fun ...' She stopped at a sharp nudge from her husband.

'The cellar's enough to be going on with,' he said. 'You'll be surprised at the volume and variety of stock we keep and, uh, of course, you'll be responsible for the ordering and restocking.'

'After consultation with us,' added Katie hastily.

'Oh yes, you'll have to keep an eye on me.' Martin's tone was frosty. Did she think he was going to plunder the cellar?

'Well, it's because we understand about the turnover in certain lines,' chipped in Peter. 'We don't want to order too much of anything and have it left on our hands. For instance, most of our customers don't care much for brown ale. We've got seven crates of the stuff down in the cellar. They've been mouldering away there since 1898.'

Martin said nothing and there was an embarrassed pause. Feeling somewhat awkward, Peter turned to his wife.

'How about some pud then, Katie? Can't send a man to work on an empty stomach.'

NINETEEN

'I had no idea your friend was so wealthy. She agreed to the original price without hesitation. I thought I would have to come down at least £500 to find a buyer. She must want it very much.' Gerald Strickland settled his corpulent self in an armchair and lit a fat cigar. 'Damn good profit,' he murmured, watching the fragrant smoke curl up into the air. 'It'll go some way to recompense me for keeping your misfit husband all these years.'

His daughter looked peevishly at him. 'What about me? I haven't got my own house any more.'

Gerald's face clouded with irritation. 'For God's sake, Helen. I offered you the house and you said you could never be happy there again. You only had to ask and I would have made you a gift of it. Don't be so damned contrary. And anyway, surely you realise that if you were living there he would certainly try to move in with you again. After the way he's been behaving I think you're safer here. The truth is, I was thinking of putting the profit on this sale into trust for Rosalie. Surely you're pleased about that?'

'You sold it before I had time to think ...'

'Dammit girl, you've had three weeks to think and all you do is whine that you don't understand such things and need a man to decide for you. Well I'm a man and I've decided. One does not turn down such a good offer.'

Helen jabbed the needle angrily into her embroidery and tugged the silk through, tangling it and wrinkling the cloth. Then she paused and stared at her father as the long-suspended penny dropped.

'But she's not!'

'Not what?' sighed Gerald.

'Wealthy! I remember the time I first met her. She said quite distinctly that she could not afford to stay at the Maple for very much longer. That was when I invited her to Forest Rift.' Helen sounded outraged.

'The lady has paid in cash.'

'Cash?' shrieked Helen. 'But why would she say ...? I mean, why give the impression that one is hard up when it's not true? After all, poverty is nothing to be proud of.'

'It sounds to me as though she was angling for an invitation—which you duly supplied. What does it matter now, anyway?'

His daughter's lip trembled. 'I'll never have my own home again. I'm too old to find another husband,' she quavered. 'I'm middle-aged and no one will want me.'

'Divorce is becoming a little more common, you know. It's not such a stigma any more if that's what's worrying you.'

'I don't care about that!' Helen flung the needlework across the room. 'It's my age that bothers me! I've got crow's-feet already.'

'I hope you're not considering reconciliation with that wretch.'

'No, no, no!' howled Helen. 'I want another man.'

'Well you still have a great many admirers, and who knows, after a decent interval one of them may ...'

'They're all bloody married,' she snapped.

'Language!'

Gerald felt a twinge of despair at the prospect of trying to marry Helen off a second time, in middle age and with a ten-year-old daughter. He had rather hoped she would accept her single state and take up knitting. His motives were partly selfish, for Gerald had been a widower for nearly twenty years and the presence of Helen and Rosalie in his house did a great deal to relieve the loneliness.

'Well,' he said reluctantly, 'we'll have some parties this winter and you can have a complete new wardrobe.'

The sobbing magically ceased. 'Oh Papa, you've always been so good to me,' Helen burbled, 'and I've got a wonderful idea. Someone's started a motor enthusiasts' club in Stennack. Why don't we invite them along? I'm sure I could make lots of new friends.'

'Perhaps. We'll see.'

Helen knew that this meant yes. It had always been the same; what she wanted she got.

'Peter says that Martin's quite an adequate worker,' she said, suddenly switching the subject.

'Just adequate? I suppose that's all one can expect.'

'Of course, they're not paying him,' she went on, retrieving the embroidery, 'and he's not always very gracious when asked to do something but on the whole they're pleasantly surprised.'

'I wouldn't have given him a job,' grunted the old man. 'I wouldn't have him under my roof.' He tossed the cigar butt into the fireplace. 'No damn' good.'

A vague sensation of guilt swept over Helen, remembering the note she had sent to Peter. There was no denying the way she had played down her own misbehaviour whilst enlarging on Martin's. But then that was only natural, wasn't it? A girl had to take care of herself.

'I wonder if he knows about the house?' she mused.

'That I've sold it? He'll hear sooner or later. News travels like a bushfire around here. I imagine he'll be none too pleased to hear who's bought it.'

'Hmm. It came as a shock to me,' agreed Helen.

Her thoughts wandered, vaguely tracing some connection, some pattern that had eluded her since the day she learned that Forest Rift now belonged to Laurel Jay. Even Helen's fuddled mind had formed an impression that somehow things had begun to go wrong almost from the day that Laurel came to Forest Rift. The family balance, that unspoken compromise on which so many relationships exist, had begun to topple when ... Yes, when exactly? Surely from the day she met Conran? Or was it before?

'I'm glad Rosie hasn't been upset by all this.' Gerald's voice interrupted her thoughts.

Helen sniffed. 'She was never very close to Martin, so she doesn't miss him. Most of the time he ignored her.' Helen omitted to confess that she had no time for Rosie either.

'I like having her here,' Gerald said contentedly. 'She brings a bit of life into the house and at least she's got some little friends now.'

The Stricklands' neighbours had three boisterous children—twin boys of ten and a nine-year-old daughter—who were glad to have Rosalie for a playmate. The old man always marvelled at his granddaughter's resilience in view of her turbulent home life and part of him hoped desperately that Helen would not remarry and uproot the child again.

'I did tell you, didn't I, that you and Rosie have an invitation to Forest Rift at any time. I know Mrs Jay would be pleased to see you. After all, she doesn't have a lot of close friends.'

Helen considered for a moment. 'Well, we always did get on together and Rosie simply loves her. Just like a sister. I must say, Laurel was a comfort to me when Michael ran off. I expect I'll call and see her sometime next week.'

'Exactly. You would be foolish to lose contact with all your old friends just because your marriage has failed.'

Gerald immediately regretted his lack of tact, for her eyes filled as if ready for another outburst of self-pity. She choked it back however and contented herself with a muffled sob, dabbing her eyes with a dainty hanky.

'I still can't understand,' she sniffed, 'where Laurel got the money.'

Forest Rift's new owner wandered thoughtfully from room to room. None of it was new to her. The house had just seemed to slip into her possession. There was no sensation of having seized it, no surge of triumph, just a quiet satisfaction.

It came complete with carpets and furnishings, most of which she decided to keep. Some of the linen, curtains and covers were not to her taste but on the whole there was little to be changed.

Naturally she would have to engage new staff for the house. Only Gil and Jacob remained of the old crew and Mrs Jay had special plans for them.

She wondered why, even if his daughter didn't want it, Gerald had not kept Forest Rift for himself. It seemed incredible that anyone should want to be rid of such a beautiful place. But then Gerald was a banker and she was an artist. Their priorities differed widely—which was convenient for Laurel, longing as she was to own this house and land. It deserved appreciation, needed someone to preserve its gentle atmosphere and restore some calm after the tumult of the past few weeks.

She had a sudden sharp vision of Helen and Martin, grown old here together. Helen without her looks and her admirers to cushion the emptiness of life, Martin sour, resentful and bored. There would have been no mellowing for those two when the rest of the world withdrew—as it often does in old age—leaving them alone together, like two irascible chickens constantly stabbing at each other.

The hall clock chimed 3.15 and she was expecting a girl to interview for the position of cook at four o'clock. She went up to her bedroom and selected a reasonably businesslike dress of dark brown, relieved by dainty white lace at the collar and cuffs. A touch of innocence, she thought, observing herself in the mirror. White for purity, white for the angels. Her eyes opened wide in the youthful, ingenuous way she had practised to perfection. The harmless stare that so often accompanied a barbed remark. That 'please-don't-misunderstand-me' look. Then the expression faded as her mouth curved into the gleaming, predatory grin which truly belonged to Laurel Jay, and her eyes creased lazily at the corners. They were green.

TWENTY

The gloom of winter had settled heavily on Martin Warbeck. He had now spent nine miserable weeks as cellarman at the Maple House and as yet Helen showed no signs of relenting. Hope faded week by week as she pressed on with the divorce proceedings and he began to fear that this captivity, this forced labour, would go on indefinitely. His anger at learning the identity of Forest Rift's new owner had long since subsided, replaced by a dismal depression, a kind of inertia which made his work doubly demanding, since it was an effort to move at all. His dull mood had robbed him even of the solace he once found in hating and blaming the whole world for his plight. All of a sudden hate required too much energy and he simply couldn't be bothered.

Christmas had been exhausting and there

was still the New Year's Eve party to get through. Day by day his misery deepened and it seemed that nothing would ever interest him again—until the parcel came.

It sat on his dresser for two days before he bothered to open it. Such was the depth of his apathy. Finally, just before going to bed on the second night, he began carelessly ripping away the wrapping. Inside was a box. A wooden box, perhaps a foot square, with a hinged lid. He flipped back the catch and opened it. Inside, a layer of tissue was spread across the top and something glinted underneath. Something metallic. Silver? He put his hand in and drew out the object, shaking away the remainder of the packing.

Like a precious little ghost, the horse seemed to glow with the eeriness of the long lost. Something returned from time. Something of great significance.

Stung with shock, Martin nearly dropped it. He turned it round, gingerly, as if it might turn to dust. The horse was in perfect condition, polished and well cared for, its mother-of-pearl wings shining varicoloured in the firelight.

How? Who? And, most important, why? He rummaged in the box for some letter or note, the name of the sender, and found a small white card, such as any florist might use. It said simply, 'Memento.'

Martin turned it over. Nothing. He tossed it away and searched once more through the packing. No, nothing. Just the one word, 'Memento.' To his blemished conscience the implication was fearfully clear. He was not pleased to receive the horse, no matter what it might be worth. Its arrival was a threat and a resurrection of grim memories.

There was no sleep for him that night, just tossing and worried conjecture. They were after him and this was advance warning, to torment him, make him sweat. The Shea family had not, after all, forgotten Rachel. He got up twice to make sure his door and windows were bolted. It never occurred to Martin that the horse might be simply a taunt. He was convinced there was worse to follow and spent the most miserable night since the trap incident.

At breakfast the next day he looked altogether haggard and ate almost nothing. The Stricklands noticed that he seemed preoccupied and nervous. In an oblique attempt to find out why, Katie accidentally went straight to the cause.

'Have you opened your parcel?'

Martin looked startled.

'It's just that I was dusting your room yesterday and I noticed that you still hadn't ...' she faltered. 'I didn't mean to be nosy.'

There was a lengthy silence, then he said, 'As a matter of fact I have opened it. It's a—present—from a friend. Something rather special. Valuable.'

'Belated Christmas present?'

'No, no, nothing like that.'

Peter stared at him from under his thick eyebrows. 'Not your birthday, is it? You should have told us.'

'No, it's, uh, something I had coming to me. Something I'd forgotten until now.' He seemed to be searching out and choosing his words carefully. Peter looked puzzled.

'Really? I had no idea it was important. It didn't come by special post or anything.'

Martin, alerted, looked from one to the other. 'How did it come?' he asked eagerly.

'By hand. That young fellow brought it. The one who used to work for you,' answered Katie.

'The stablehand?'

'That's the one. He's got a brother who's not quite right, poor soul. What's his name, Pete? The younger one?'

'Gil, isn't it?' Peter looked to Martin for confirmation but he wasn't listening. A suspicion was taking shape in his mind, confused but groping in the right direction.

'Did he say anything?'

'Not a murmur, just handed me the parcel.'

'Um, I've got to, uh, make a start.' Martin pushed his chair back and got up.

'Yes, make room for today's delivery.'

'We don't have a delivery on Thursdays.'

'What? Oh, no, well, I'll be getting on anyway.'

Peter watched him hurry off down to

the cellar and shot a curious glance at his wife.

'First time I've known him so anxious to start work.'

'Positively keen.'

'Something is bothering him.'

'About his parcel?'

'So it seems.'

'Peter, if he's got a bit of capital you could offer him ...'

'Oh no, Kate. I don't want a partner. You know what that would mean. We'd be liable for any debts he incurred and anyway the old man wouldn't hear of it. He's got money in this place too, you know.'

'I just thought you'd know how to make it work for him. After all, he hasn't got much sense over money and I hoped you could suggest some safe ideas—you know, investments.'

'I'm not going to mention it.'

'But if he asks you ...?'

'Somehow I don't think he will. Now let's drop the subject, eh?'

'He's learnt a lot,' she went on. 'Perhaps

he's changed and this is the opportunity he needs to set himself right again.'

'What are you, his guardian angel? Why are you so keen to supervise his recovery? You soon forget, don't you? I wouldn't trust Martin with his own daughter's piggy-bank and I'm certainly not having him financially involved with us. And what about the way he treated Helen, eh?'

'I don't hold grudges,' retorted Katie stiffly. 'I just thought he deserved a chance, that's all.'

'Well I'll think it over. Maybe Pa will have some bright ideas as to how he can invest it. I've given him a job and that's all I'm prepared to do.'

'You want to keep him as a cellarman for the rest of his life?'

'Oh don't be ridiculous. Since when was I vindictive? If something better crops up for him elsewhere then I'll wish him luck, but I don't think he's got what it takes to be a success on his own and it's certainly not my duty to rehabilitate him.'

Katie, aware that Martin was, as she had always feared, in danger of upsetting their happy lives, resolved not to continue the argument with her husband.

'Sorry,' she said quietly, 'I shouldn't have said that.'

'Oh let's forget it. He'll probably lose the lot when the Grand National rolls round.'

Martin's mind was not on partnerships, investments or anything monetary. He needed peace and quiet to sort out his ideas; peace which he found sitting atop a keg of bitter at the far end of the cellar where he had stacked a number of empty crates to form a little cubicle in the corner. Here he could sit and smoke, downing a few pints of ale between jobs. Peter knew about it and said nothing. He would expect the same of any cellarman and was gratified that Martin kept his hands off the more expensive stuff.

Gil had delivered the parcel. Gil who still worked at Forest Rift—for Laurel Jay. That girl had come into his life like a streak of bad luck and now, as a gift from her, came this other bringer of trouble. He shuddered at the memories evoked by the statuette.

His fright however had quite disappeared. She was, after all, only a woman. Aside from the servants, he thought, she must be quite alone out there and a visit to the lady might be very instructive.

The sad drawback of quiet country places is their bleakness in winter. Rowan Water was grey and choppy. Even the house looked dull and cold, backed by the gaunt outlines of trees which dripped rainwater dejectedly onto the roof. Forest Rift had never before looked harsh to him. Perhaps it seemed so now because it was, so to speak, in enemy hands.

He trudged along the old path where he used to exercise Coriander, his boots squishing on the sodden ground. Muffled and wrapped against the east wind, he had walked all the way from Meadstock. If Laurel was not at home then he would wait until she was, but something told him that he wouldn't be turned away. The statuette was a kind of invitation and he was curious to know why.

The maid who opened the door was of course new. Martin had to repeat his name twice before she got it right and ambled off in no great hurry to announce him.

'Mrs Jay is in the study,' she said on returning. 'You can go straight in.'

Martin glowered at the maid, for she looked him up and down without a trace of respect and he heard a quiet 'hmmph' as she turned and bustled away.

Laurel had rearranged the study. He stepped inside and glared round at new drapes and ornaments. One of her own paintings hung above the fireplace.

'Like it?' She was sitting in Gordon's favourite armchair, feet crossed comfortably on the fender.

He didn't answer.

'I'm surprised it's taken you so long. I've been expecting a visit for days.' The girl was grinning, the old, taunting grin that had spoilt his temper and his digestion so many times at dinner.

'Where did you get it?' He had intended

the question as casual but it came out harsh and eager.

'The horse?'

'What else?'

Laurel chuckled.

'You bought it from someone?' he pressed.

'It was given to me.'

'By whom?'

'I think you should sit down before I tell you any more.'

Warbeck seated himself on the settee and accepted a glass of port.

'My uncle gave it to me,' she said, settling herself once more in the great tapestried chair.

'And where did he get it?'

'Really, Mr Warbeck, you're being very stupid, very slow.'

Martin listened uneasily.

'You know where he got it,' she went on. 'I'm sure you can recall the incident quite clearly. I myself was only a few weeks old at the time but I've been told the story so often it almost seems as if I was there. Nevertheless I'd quite like to hear your version,' Laurel paused and her eyebrows lifted in amusement, 'Father.'

As her meaning sank in, part of his mind wondered at the sensation of dull shock. He had always been aware that the Rachel episode had left a few loose ends but this was one he had never even considered. Still he hesitated to accept the reality.

'Oh, no,' Martin half laughed and shook his head. 'There was no child. At least, none that lived. She told me, it was a boy and he was stillborn.'

'Oh you know what a liar she was!' chortled the girl. 'By all accounts, she seldom told anyone the truth about anything. After all,' she said, watching his face with enjoyment, 'she told you the horse was sold and that wasn't true either, was it?' The smile disappeared and a nasty glint appeared in her green eyes. 'That particular lie earned her more than she bargained for, didn't it?'

'I ... but, I mean, why? Why did she tell me you had died? I could have provided for you.'

Martin should have guessed that this wouldn't work but confusion dulled his wits.

'Ah, well, that's the whole point, isn't it? Providing for me. Taking responsibility for one's offspring. In normal circumstances a father provides everything for his child. He feeds it, clothes it, supplies every need. But without the fine ceremony, the sanction of some clergyman and the law, father can escape such burdens entirely, can't he? Smug society will censure the mother but excuse him with a mild 'tut-tut'. Now isn't that right? Shall I call you Papa, by the way? Would you like that?'

He could find nothing to say.

'Rachel, however, attempted to provide for me in her own muddlesome way,' continued Laurel. She sighed. 'I don't think poor mother was especially clever. Myself, I'm a little more intelligent—which is just about the only gift I ever received from you.' A look of sudden contempt flicked across her face. 'A hundred pounds and an ornament—albeit an expensive ornament.

You drowned her for something as petty as that.'

'It was an accident. I only meant to frighten her.' Panic tinged his voice. 'You don't understand what happened. I had to get the horse back. I even offered her the money if she'd let me have the horse but she said it was sold ...'

'I know what she said,' answered Laurel sharply. 'Alec heard that much. It was only a joke—surely you realised that? As for trying to frighten her, she could have drowned twice over in the time you kept her under. Is your judgement that bad?'

'I was upset, I couldn't help ...' stammered Martin. 'It was because of my father. He was going to cut me out of his will. That horse belonged to him, it was special to him and he thought I had taken it.'

'Why? Why should he think that?'

'I needed some money and he wouldn't let me have it,' muttered Martin reluctantly.

'Ah, yes, now I get the picture. But he didn't cut you out, now did he? You still got your blasted money!'

Martin groaned. 'How was I to know what would happen? As far as I knew at that moment, she had ruined me. And what is the point of all this after twenty years? Is it an apology you want?'

Laurel's good humour began to revive. 'I've never cared for apologies,' she said lightly. 'They're so inadequate—and what can you do with one when you've got it? You can't eat it or spend it or live in it. I suppose you can always gloat a little but on the whole I prefer a more substantial form of atonement. And of course,' she gestured round the room, 'I've got exactly what I want. You, on the other hand, are ruined—which is just what Alec's been waiting for all these years.'

Martin began to feel a little queasy. 'Oh yes,' he said slowly, 'Alec. What happened to him?'

Laurel smirked. 'Time for a reunion,' she said, reaching for the bell pull and tugging it twice. The same maid who had answered the front door sidled curiously into the study. 'Julie, ask Mr Shea to come in, will you?'

Martin remembered the boy who was Rachel's brother, a thin, dirty child with dark eyes and torn clothes. He had never speculated on what changes time had made to Alec Shea. Martin simply recalled him as he was and although the logical side of his mind expected to see a full grown man the shock was still more than he bargained for. Doubly so because he knew the man, knew him by another name, had entertained him at dinner and, regretfully, allowed him to entertain Helen as well.

'You scheming bastard.' The words came in a whisper.

'Conran was mother's maiden name, you know,' said Alec pleasantly. 'I think it suits me quite well.'

'Alec's changed a lot, hasn't he? I hear he was quite scraggy as a child but he's developed some muscle since then,' purred Laurel.

He certainly had. It had never escaped Martin's notice that Conran was stronger and fitter than he was. Understanding crashed in on him as the puzzle rearranged itself and locked into place.

'You did this between you, broke up my marriage, you've cost me ...'

'Just about everything,' finished Alec. 'I truly am sorry about Helen but I'm sure she'll get over it.'

'It was you, you left that thing in my room and dropped the slate through the roof.' Martin's gaze turned to the girl.

'Guilty,' chuckled Laurel. 'I never intended to do you any serious damage—of course. I wouldn't be so crude, or so inefficient. You were much too quick to accuse poor old Helen. She thinks you're mad, you know. Quite, quite crazy.'

'You made everything so easy,' continued Shea. 'If you had possessed any degree of self-sufficiency, were not dependent on Helen for everything, we would have found it much harder to bring you down.'

'Yes, in a way you quite spoilt our fun,' agreed Laurel.

'I think you're both taking altogether too much credit,' snapped Martin. 'There were other circumstances in this mess which had nothing to do with you.'

'True, although Cordelia's new husband owes me some thanks for the time I spent dictating love-letters to the lady.' Alec grinned as Warbeck's jaw dropped. 'Devoted but shy, that's Coleman. The poor devil had been hankering after Cordey for years, without any luck. He didn't propose in person, you know. He sent her a letter. I had to dictate that one too.'

'I think, to be fair, Alec, we must admit an element of luck,' said Laurel. 'But,' she added, turning to Martin, 'if you had not made yourself so unpopular with everyone you might not be in your present position. We'd have had to think of something else. You see, you're much too fond of abusing people.'

Martin's face looked chalky. 'I bet you two took years to work this out,' he said faintly.

'Not at all,' answered the girl brightly. 'I mean, on the whole we didn't know much about you. I had not the faintest idea what to do until I really got talking to your wife.

You know how she chatters on, lets things slip. It didn't take me so very long to form a picture of the situation.'

'And you've done all this just for revenge, just to see me sweat.'

Laurel considered him for a moment. 'Well, yes. After all, you did drown my mother. But, above all, I don't like being disowned. I find it insulting—you know, not good enough to acknowledge and so on. And of course I wanted this house. Cassie used to describe it to me when I was very small. It sounded so enchanting—despite its evil owner. She died, you know, just two years ago. Poor old Cass.'

'You needn't congratulate yourself,' snapped Martin. 'Strickland has made a hell of a profit on this sale. You're a pair of bloody fools.'

She dismissed that with a shrug. 'Cheap at twice the price—after all, it included the cost of your downfall.'

'And, what's more, we've not done anything that isn't legal,' added Alec.

'You call assault legal? I could have

been killed that day in the conservatory. My God, a pair of dregs like you in my house ...'

'We're rich dregs,' interrupted Alec, quite unoffended. 'I suppose you may look on us in much the same way as the old squire must have looked on your own family when you first moved in here.'

'Jumped-up,' supplied Laurel.

'That's the term,' agreed Shea. They both seemed to find his contempt very funny.

'And where did all this money come from?' sneered Martin. 'I fully expected it would go on gin and music halls.'

'Quite wrong. You see how you persistently underestimate people. Cassie took the money and started a small dress shop in a backstreet in Bath, initially using her own cloth. All very humble stuff to begin with, but that money of yours paid for a sewing-machine, among other things, which helped speed up her output. Poor dear, she worked fifteen hours a day for the first two years but of course the business built up and things got better. Now we have a large, smart shop in the centre of the city. We import dresses from Paris and half the fine birds in Bath get their feathers from us,' explained Alec. 'And as soon as I was old enough I extended the business into gentlemen's attire. It's been a terrific success.'

'Personally I'm lost in the world of trade and commerce,' purred the girl, 'but I do enjoy designing clothes.'

'I don't give a damn about your pathetic little lives,' hissed Martin.

'We know.' The humour suddenly left Shea's face. 'We are well aware that you don't give a damn about us or anyone else. It might interest you to know that in my younger days I had a perfectly serious ambition to drown you, just as you drowned Rachel.'

'Old Testament justice,' added Laurel.

'However, as my niece so rightly observes, you're really not worth it. In fact we both feel that things have gone far enough.'

'By and large, I'd say we've been fairly generous,' remarked the girl. 'I mean to say, we've given you the horse, the thing that you wanted so much. We had it valued, you know. It's worth about £400 now—which may be enough to buy you a small stake in a business. I don't think that's unfair, and who knows, you might end up as wealthy as we are—if you work round the clock, seven days a week, fifty-two weeks a year.'

Martin paled.

'You see,' she went on, 'I didn't know my mother, so I'm unable to feel quite as bitter about that as Alec does. What I resent is the fact that you didn't want anything to do with me. I've always felt that this should be my home, that I'm entitled to live here, if you know what I mean. So now I do live here and I'm satisfied.'

'It was never my idea to let you have that statuette back,' said Alec. 'I'd never have offered you a penny but Laurel seems curious to know if you're capable of making something out of it. Forgiving, isn't she?'

Martin decided he had had enough. He

had listened thus far out of miserable curiosity and now that he understood everything his most urgent wish was to get away from these two gloating young people. He got unsteadily to his feet.

'Oh you're not going, are you?' exclaimed the girl. 'We were enjoying it so much.'

Martin stared mutely from one to the other, loathing their smiling faces.

'I suppose you can find your own way out?' joked Alec. 'Not forgotten your way around yet?'

The other man hardly heard. He turned and shuffled dazedly from the room and out of the house. A kind of stupor settled on him as he trudged back along the path to town. It was all too much to think about just then, too painful. One thought however lodged clearly in his head; that this was logical and inevitable. How intensely silly of him to think he had got away with it! Murder was never simple, not even for a rich man. There was always a price and always someone to collect the debt.

TWENTY-ONE

Martin sold the horse, not only for need of the money, but because of its depressing associations. It fetched £370, which was quite a healthy sum in those days. He could have bought a small house with it and perhaps taken a lodger. Even Gerald, after some deliberation, offered him the benefit of his experience and suggested a few safe investments which would bring him a useful little dividend each year. It was, as Katie had said, a chance and he could make of it what he wished. Gerald, still sceptical, wondered if that would be anything much. It was like offering a new trick to an old dog and Strickland had his doubts.

The upturn in his fortunes didn't appear to have improved Martin's temper at all. His thoughts dwelt continually on the girl at Forest Rift and the more he brooded on it, the angrier he got. His daughter! Dear God! It had never occurred to him that there might after all have been a child. At the time it had seemed quite natural for Rachel to lose the baby after the beating he gave her. It was a logical consequence and not to be questioned. Martin had been only too ready to believe it. He was also disturbed and frightened to realise that yokels like the Sheas could sustain a grudge for the space of twenty years and visit such calculated and effective revenge upon him.

He was unable to simply accept the situation and allow them their satisfaction. His misfortunes seemed so much worse since he had discovered the cause of them but the more he searched for a way to hit back, the more helpless he felt. He could not prove they had done anything illegal, nor could he ask anyone's advice or explain the situation without raking up the whole sorry tale of Rachel Shea.

On the Tuesday of the third week in January there was a heavy fall of snow. Everything froze. Dense twelve-foot drifts cut off villages and hamlets, buried sheep and stopped all deliveries to the Maple House.

'I hope the bitch freezes. I hope she's got no coal, no kindling, no food out there,' Martin muttered to himself that morning as he sat shivering on top of his beer keg in the cellar and downed a pint of stout in lieu of breakfast. He feared it was a vain hope, for Forest Rift was always amply stocked with everything. At least it had been so in his day. He doubted that the likes of her would know how to run such a house. After all, she was only trash. Martin still managed to avoid acknowledging to himself that she was a blood relative, every bit as much his daughter as Rosie was. He preferred to think of her as 'Rachel's brat'.

No one came in that lunchtime. Not even the regular heavy drinkers would risk a broken leg or worse on the streets, where snow had hardened into a thick veil of ice and the slightest lapse of care was apt to send a man sprawling on his back. The cold was bone-deep and even indoors waves of chill seemed to ripple through the body from time to time.

There was nothing for Martin to do. He sat morosely behind the bar, polishing some brasses, until quarter past one when Peter decided to offer him the day off. Martin grabbed the opportunity and scurried off to the sanctuary of his room.

One of the worst things about work, he'd found, was the way it interfered with one's thinking. It was difficult to brood on things when people and jobs needed constant attention, so his problems remained there at the back of his mind, nagging to be solved, and he couldn't have peace and quiet to work things out.

He had been moved to a better room and was now getting a modest wage. Peter had softened a bit, finding his brother-in-law tolerable to work with, and he gave him a small guestroom on the south side —for the winter at least. In that room, in the wardrobe, beneath a top hat he wore only to funerals, Martin kept a bottle of Napoleon brandy.

As always, in times of frustration or

adversity, a few drinks softened reality and soothed the unpleasant churning of his own inward anger. Sometimes they even provided inspiration.

It was all wrong that she should be out there, living in his house, laughing at him. His marriage to Helen seemed suddenly wonderful and he began to think of them in maudlin terms as the good old days. Everything had been cosy and he wanted it back, just as it was. To hell with his lousy few hundred pounds. This was an insult when one was used to a fortune. A handout, he thought, a paltry little handout. And from her! Of all people! Did she expect him to be grateful? Oh, if only he hadn't upset Helen and if only ...

'Cordey,' he whimpered, 'how could you pull such a dirty trick?' His face clouded as he squinted at the fire, mourning for Cordelia's £60,000. 'Treacherous bitch!' He suddenly flung the brandy glass at the bedroom door, where it shattered and deposited a shower of glass splinters across the floor.

Martin plonked himself clumsily on the

rug, leaning his back against the side of the bed and wriggling his toes before the fire—a habit he had brought with him from childhood. He would think of something. Sooner or later. If only Alec Shea was not there to look after dear Laurel. If only he could get her alone there would be some justice done.

January 30th arrived and it was a Thursday. Most of the main roads were now clear, the towns and villages freed of their crippling blankets of ice, save for odd banks of discoloured slush which remained in out of the way corners. Country locations like Forest Rift were accessible at last and it was on this Thursday morning that the two brothers, Gil and Jacob, arrived in town to buy foodstuffs, lamp-oil and other supplies which had been depleted through the freeze. Not least of Mrs Jay's requirements was a supply of wines and spirits and, as a family friend, she gave her custom to Peter Strickland.

It was Martin's unwelcome task to serve them, for Peter was occupied in conversation at the bar with a wine-merchant from Bristol. Gil silently handed his former employer a list. Martin glanced from him to the timid Jacob who sidled in and hovered behind his brother, his spiky hair and watery eyes more affrighted than ever. Resentfully Martin assembled a number of bottles on the counter.

'They're all there, just as she's ordered.'

'I know,' said Gil shortly, 'I've read the list.'

'How very accomplished you are.'

Jacob, staring vacantly over his brother's shoulder, sensed antagonism and peered closely into Gil's face, seeking reassurance. The young man didn't seem to notice him. He didn't like being sneered at, having become accustomed to better treatment from Laurel Jay.

'Aye, I am too. You'd be amazed at the extent of my education. Especially where horses are concerned. Mrs Jay's been talking about breeding them, now that she's settled in at the house. Did you know that?'

Warbeck's eyes widened.

'So she'll be needing a man who knows a bit about them, maybe even a partner.' Gil allowed himself a smirk of satisfaction. 'Imagine, Mr Warbeck, the day may come when I'll be a rich man.'

'You can't do that, not out there. You don't have the space or the stabling,' sneered Martin.

'Did I say we were using Forest Rift? Now did I? Mrs Jay has it in mind to buy Dewi Purling's stables, over at Stennack, and some of the fine land round abouts. Exciting, isn't it?'

'She's mad. Stupid bloody woman, she doesn't know a thing about horses.'

'Ah, but it was Mr Conran's idea, you see, and he does know quite a bit, if you recall. Met him at the racetrack, didn't you? You must have wondered where he got his tips from. It seems that he and Mrs Jay have become business partners all of a sudden.'

'But he's a tailor!' exclaimed Martin indignantly.

'Not exactly. It's true that he owns a number of ladies' dress shops and gents' outfitters, but he's involved in one or two other things as well, including horse breeding. I hear he's got a large stud in Somerset.'

'And what makes you think they'll want you as a partner? You haven't got any money to put into their stupid little venture.'

Martin was becoming desperately angry, groping for some flaw in the arrangement, something to spoil Gil's hopes.

'It's not a question of money. It's a matter of time and know-how,' replied the stablehand. 'Mr Conran can't be down here all the time. He's got his business in Bath to think about—and besides I don't think he wants to fall foul of your wife.'

'Really? He appears to have deserted all that in favour of country life—or is it simply that these impressive businesses don't exist?'

'Oh, they exist all right. As a matter of fact he went back to Bath last night. Idleness,' added Gil with emphasis, 'is not one of his faults.'

He picked up three of the bottles and

handed them to his brother, who took them gingerly at first, then cradled them fiercely to his chest, knowing in his idiot's way that on no account must he drop them.

'Put them in the trap—careful now,' explained his brother patiently and the excited Jacob scurried obediently outside. Between them they shifted the consignment of drink out to the trap and Martin watched it drive off. The muscles of his face felt heavy. They ached with the effort of sustaining a mask of composure when he felt so wretched.

Horses? Her? Gil a partner? It was the very thing that he, Martin, had always wanted—stables. Ever since he could remember he had wanted stables like Purling had, but no one had ever offered to buy him any. It seemed to Martin that he was to be the only loser in this whole affair.

He groaned and looked at his pocket watch. It was 12.15. He could go soon, and have a few hours to himself, for Thursday was his half-day.

An hour later, free, he slouched off to his room to chew over this latest news. Did the future hold such prosperity for Laurel Jay? For Gil? For everyone, it seemed, except himself. This was intolerable, unbearable, and it shouldn't be permitted.

He pulled open his wardrobe and took out the bottle. It was two thirds full. Fifteen fluid ounces of comfort, anaesthesia and, yes, courage too.

It took him just over an hour to empty that bottle. His head lolled, every limb heavy, and a sober fraction of his mind noted that he had never swallowed so much so quickly before. Must be a record, something remarkable. But then, surely, he was in every way remarkable, wasn't he? Attractive, clever. Yes, clever. His schoolteachers had said so, long years ago. They were unanimous in their praise: a good mathematical brain, an excellent command of English, superb general knowledge. A good all-rounder, eh? And the women admired him—his looks, his social position ...

'What social position?' screamed reality.

'You're just a barman with a few hundred pounds that won't last six months. Once you were worth thousands and thousands. Boundless money—or so it seemed. In the end what use was it to be so academically smart? Perhaps if you had been gifted with a little more common sense, a little less conceit ...' Martin found these thoughts disagreeable and abruptly switched them off.

There would have been more. He glared at his reflection in the wardrobe mirror and lifted the bottle, draining it to the last drip. More money. Not just a third of the Warbeck wealth but three-quarters at least. Neil and Celia would never have had so much if it hadn't been for that thieving, common tramp, Rachel Shea. It always came down to her in the end. And now here was her daughter. Another Rachel, another grasping little whore. Not his daughter, not Rosie's half-sister. Laurel was part of Rachel Shea. If you turned that black hair red she would be Rachel Shea.

His arms clasped around his knees, he

rocked back and forth, half-crying, half-snarling. Poor Martin. It wasn't fair. They had taken his home away, his fortune, everything. And whose fault was it? That wily, green-eyed witch.

Alec Shea had gone back to Bath. He was out of reach—two hundred miles away. Well, that was all right. Martin wasn't too sure how to deal with him anyway, but Laurel was a simple matter. She deserved just what her mother had got and now was as good a time as any. Now, when he felt, in his alcoholic fog, angry enough and crazy enough. He lurched to his feet, struggled into his outdoor coat. There would be no horses and no prosperity for her. He'd make bloody sure.

Martin stumbled down the stairs, out through the delivery entrance and across the green, which was still overlaid with ice. He slipped through the churchyard and into the lane, the path that led eventually to Forest Rift.

TWENTY-TWO

He hit the ground with a jarring thump which left him quite breathless. How many times was that? Four or five? With a bit more caution he need not have fallen at all, for the thaw was under way and the ice was avoidable, broken by large patches of clear ground. Martin however was in a hurry and he charged straight on. The effects of the brandy and a northeast wind had combined to give him a fearful headache but he was halfway sober again by this time and quite clear in his mind that he was going to get the bitch, although not exactly sure how. He had covered nearly two miles and had come to the northern end of the woodland path. Not far now.

Rowan Water was still frozen from shore to shore and a few hardy wildfowl could be seen making breakneck landings on the ice, their expansive, webbed feet splayed out before them as braking power. And they were not the only ones out on the frozen surface.

Martin halted, peering through the trees. A small, obviously female figure had just pushed off from the jetty and was making hesitant progress towards the centre of the ice.

He watched her strides lengthen as she gained confidence, watched her attempt a few cautious turns. She was just proficient enough on skates to amuse herself, but slipped once or twice, landing on her behind with a little shriek. Martin grinned, his eyes following every movement. It was good that she was out of the house, made things that much easier. If she kept going in the same direction she would soon be out of sight of Forest Rift, blocked out by the same belt of trees which had covered the drowning of her mother. He darted along the bank, hidden by the undergrowth, keeping pace with her meandering movements. She was getting farther and farther from the house but she kept to the centre of the lake, never closer than a hundred yards. He couldn't follow her out there without skates and hope to catch her. It was frustrating. The opportunity would be perfect if only she would come close enough. Hoping each time she veered towards him and fuming when she turned away again, Martin kept following.

The girl was wearing a long woolly coat and a blue tam with matching mittens, obviously enjoying herself despite the odd tumble. Across the stillness he could hear the swish and slice of the blades and see her awkwardly trying a figure-eight.

Fifteen minutes crawled by. He was losing patience. She would be turning back soon and the chance would be lost. He would have to find some other way ...

Then suddenly she was closer. Zig-zagging, turning, but heading gradually towards the bank. He guessed she was no more than ten yards out and wondered if he could cross those few feet of ice before she saw him and had time to bolt. Laurel drifted a few feet nearer still—and then stopped, her back half-turned to him, looking down at something. It had to be now.

She began to bend, reaching for her boot, when a flash of movement from the bank caught her eye. Jerking upright, her face taut with fright, she realised who it was and what he intended.

There were perhaps three seconds in which she saw him, understood and considered which way to run. Three seconds in which he covered eight or nine feet from the bank, slipping, lurching, hands outstretched, clawlike, reaching for her. And then the sound. A sharp and brittle gunshot crack as shards of ice flew into the air, slapped down a few feet distant and slithered along the surface. A gurgling, watery whoosh as the man, with the briefest gasp of horror, slid under and disappeared. For a moment one hand clawed for support but, stung by the jagged edges of the ice, soon released its grip.

There was another, quieter crack as a strip of ice fifteen or twenty feet long slowly collapsed along the line of the bank to left and right. The thaw was further advanced than anyone had guessed.

The first sensation that struck him as the shock subsided and he felt himself sinking was of hellish, aching cold in his temples. The next was terror. The bank shelved steeply here and he was floundering in about ten feet of water. He had drifted out under the ice and as he fought his way up he saw above him, through frosted white, the long dark shadow of the girl. He drove a hand upwards against the ice cover, as much a gesture of violence towards her as an attempt to break through. The movement pushed him further down, he rolled over and now, his sense of direction lost, there was neither time nor breath for another try.

Laurel watched, stunned, waiting for him to surface. Surely he would see the light above him and find his way out? It was only much later that she realised how the shock must have confused and disabled him.

Water sloshed over the edges of the break and ran along the ice. Any second he would come up. Laurel framed herself to run as soon as he appeared. But the water settled in the gap, the churning stopped. No sound.

She whirled round, convinced for a moment that he had somehow swum underneath, made a hole and come up behind her, that his hand was just inches from the back of her neck. But there was nothing except the bare, white expanse of Rowan Water. Nobody there.

The girl backed a yard or two from the bank. He had almost reached her. Three more steps ... Yes, oh God, yes! Three more steps. If she herself had taken those steps towards shore the ice would have done his work for him. A chill spread through her, diffusing outwards from inside, for that was just what she would have done. Laurel stared down at her broken bootlace and remembered her intention to sit on the bank, tie the ends and rethread it.

In the past any suggestion that Martin's attempt to kill her would instead save her and cost him his own life might have appealed to Laurel's sense of irony. But there was no humour in this and no satisfaction.

She stood for a long time, watching a thin layer of ice fragments form in the stretch of grey water along the lakeshore and remembering the hate in his face, turning to shock and dismay as the ice gave way beneath him.

'Why is she so upset? What makes her stand there by the window, gazing down to the water with those worried eyes? Why does she pace from room to room and look so very drained? He was nothing to her. It was no one's fault. Just another of his drunken accidents. They didn't even like each other and yet she seems to be harbouring some kind of grief? Is that the word? Conflict, confusion? Something I can't quite grasp. I understand why Neil is upset, why the in-laws are embarrassed and why Helen doesn't give a damn. But not this. It's as if she'd lost one of her own.'

Gil frowned as he watched her from beneath his eyebrows, his hands busy with the job of oiling and polishing a saddle. She was quite unaware of him, her back turned, staring absently through the window as her fingers picked at the frayed lace edging of a handkerchief. Her expression flickered and changed as the thoughts ran on, jumbled and fretful.

'I never intended this. I never meant that he should die. I thought it was over, settled. We had our fun, got what we wanted ... But it was his own fault! All of it! From start to finish, damn him. He came after me, he came to kill me. Couldn't stand losing. Did I think he would just accept it? I suppose I did. Stupid of me. Maybe we pushed him too far ... But he deserved it! He did! God only knows why I should suffer this creeping sense of guilt over him. Papa, Father—those words don't mean anything. He was just a man who owed me something. Alec would call me a fool for brooding on it. I know he would and he's usually right.'

'What do you think then? Didn't I tell you it would come up beautiful?'

Laurel looked round. 'What?'

'This old saddle. All it wanted was a bit of elbow-grease.'

She nodded. 'It's looking grand. Whose was it?'

'Neil's. He never used it much.'

'No, he's not the outdoor type.'

'Nor are you these days.'

Laurel shrugged.

'You've not been out since last Wednesday,' continued Gil. 'Why don't you come for a ride?'

'Now?'

'Of course.'

Laurel considered for a moment, then, 'Yes, I'd like that. Give me ten minutes to change.'

'Good. I'll bring the horses round.'

She waited for him in the porch, watching the waterfowl dip and glide, thankful that winter was nearly spent. When it came again, when it brought the snow and ice, then perhaps she would go away for a while, take a holiday. A strange feeling enveloped her, a kind of hollow calm, as if nothing really mattered so much after all. In a few weeks it would be spring and in months or years she might forget. But maybe not. To settle the past, you can never depend on time.

This Large Print Book for the Partially sighted, who cannot read normal print, is published under the auspices of

THE ULVERSCROFT FOUNDATION

Other MAGNA General Fiction Titles In Large Print

FRANCES ANNE BOND
Return Of The Swallow

JUDY GARDINER
All On A Summer's Day

IRIS GOWER
The Sins Of Eden

HELENE MANSFIELD
Some Women Dream

ELISABETH McNEILL
The Shanghai Emerald

ELIZABETH MURPHY
To Give And To Take

JUDITH SAXTON
This Royal Breed

Other MAGNA General Fiction Titles In Large Print

ELVI RHODES
Summer Promise

SALLY STEWART
The Women of Providence

ELISABETH McNEILL
Perseverance Place

NICHOLAS RHEA
Constable Among The Heather

JUDY TURNER
The Arcade

MISS READ
Village Affairs

PERFICK
The Darling Buds Of May